PLANET TAD

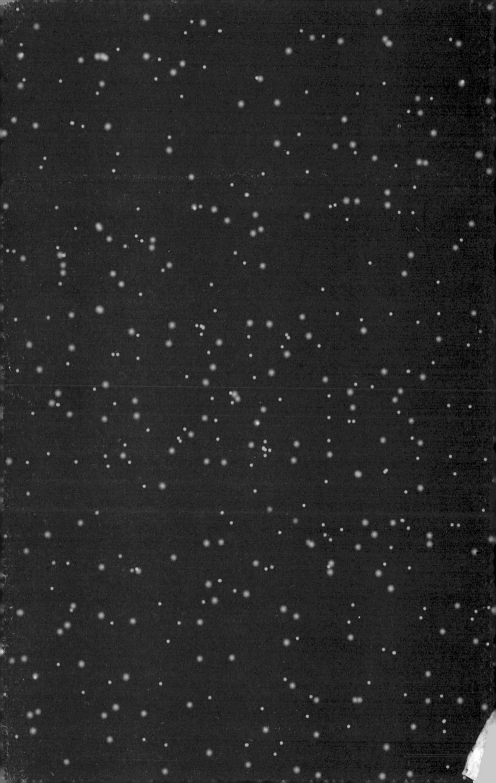

PLANET TAD

TIM CARVELL

Illustrated by Doug Holgate

MAD

HARPER

An Imprint of HarperCollinsPublishers

A portion of the text from this book
was originally published in *MAD* magazine.

Planet Tad
Copyright 2012 by E.C. Publications, Inc. All rights reserved.
MAD MAGAZINE and all related characters and elements are
trademarks of and © E.C. Publications, Inc.
(s12)
Printed in the United States of America.

Library of Congress Cataloging-in-Publication Data is available.
ISBN 978-0-06-193436-0 (trade bdg.) — ISBN 978-0-06-193437-7 (lib. bdg.)

Typography by Erin Fitzsimmons
Illustrations by Doug Holgate
Emoticons by Robert Brook Allen
12 13 14 15 16   CG/RRDH   10 9 8 7 6 5 4 3 2 1
❖
First Edition

For my mom and dad

January

Hello, world!

My name is Tad. I am twelve years old and a seventh grader at Lakeville Middle School. This is my school:

This is our mascot:

We're the Lakeville Middle School Pirates. I guess because of the "LAKEville." Although, come to think of it, you find pirates in the ocean, not in lakes. Our mascot's, like, some kind of a lame lake pirate.

The more I think about it, the more I realize that our mascot sucks.

Anyway, this is my new blog, which I am starting today, on the new computer I got for Christmas. (It's actually my dad's old computer—he got a new computer and let me have his old one. Not that I'm complaining. There are some things you can't use and then give someone else—like underwear or toothbrushes—but I don't think computers are one of them.)

I've decided to start a blog because I have a lot of important thoughts to share with the world, and also to try and get Natalie Portman to go out with me.

I'm just kidding about that last part. Although if you are Natalie Portman, and you're reading this— like, if you Googled yourself or something—hi.

I live in Lakeville with my parents and my little sister, Sophie. She's seven years old. She's OK, even though she's not as good at sneaking up on me as she thinks she is. For instance, right now, I can tell she's STANDING RIGHT BEHIND ME READING

OVER MY SHOULDER. HI, SOPHIE!

(Just heard her trip over something as she ran out of my room. Awesome.)

Starting this blog is one of my five New Year's resolutions. The other four are:

1. finish seventh grade
2. figure out how to do a kickflip on my skateboard
3. get girls to notice me
4. finally start shaving

So: One down, four to go!

JANUARY 2   [mood: annoyed]

Ugh. I can't concentrate. Sophie's in her room, practicing for her oboe recital Friday night. She's been playing the same five-minute song over and over for an hour, and it's not even a good song.

Actually, on second thought, I don't think there's such a thing as a good oboe song.

My best friend, Chuck, came over tonight to hang out. He saw that I got a new computer, and asked me what games I have. We poked around on it, but because it's my dad's computer, it doesn't really have any games on it. Still, it's got Photoshop, so we spent a little while playing around with that. For instance, this is what Sophie would look like if she had the head of a dinosaur:

I call her Sophie Rex. I think it's an improvement.

 [mood: distracted] **JANUARY 4**

Bad news: Sophie found a printout of Sophie Rex and showed it to my parents. They say that I'm not allowed to Photoshop pictures of Sophie anymore.

Of course, they didn't say anything about Photoshopping pictures of THEM:

They looked really beautiful on their wedding day.

I wonder if spiders have their own version of Spider-Man, where a spider gets bitten by a radioactive human and winds up being able to read and balance his checkbook.

Tonight, my parents made me go to Sophie's oboe recital. On our way in, I picked up a program and saw that Sophie would be playing "My Heart Will Go On" from *Titanic*. I looked at my parents and whispered, "Did you know that's the song she's been practicing for the last month?" My dad said, "Nope!" and my mom said, "Never would've guessed it in a million years." And then they made me promise to tell Sophie that she'd done a great job.

Afterward, we went out to dinner, and my dad ordered the spaghetti and meatballs, and I ordered the same thing. The waitress said, "All right. You'll have the pasketti and meatballs." And I said, "No. Spaghetti." And she said, "You're thirteen and under, right?" And I said, "I'm twelve." And she said, "Well, if you're thirteen and under, you can order from the children's menu, where it's spelled 'pasketti.'" And then she whispered, "Look: If you say 'pasketti,' it's three dollars cheaper." And I said, "I'm not going to mispronounce 'spaghetti' on purpose." And my dad said, "Come on, Tad." And I said, "I'm ordering the spaghetti and meatballs for you. If it's worth three dollars to you to have to say 'pasketti and meatballs,' you can order it for me." And my dad thought about it for a second, and then he said, "We'll have two orders of spaghetti and meatballs, please."

JANUARY 8 [mood: embarrassed]

I've been doing the Sudoku puzzle in our newspaper for a year now, and I just found out that *Sudoku* is a Japanese word. Which made me feel stupid, because for all this time, I've thought the puzzles were called Sudoku because they were made by a woman named Sue Doku. I even imagined what she looks like: She's sixty and lives alone with a whole lot of cats, and she spends her days filling in grids of numbers, then erasing almost all of them.

When Chuck came to school today, he asked me, "So, you notice anything different?" I looked at him for a while, and the only thing I noticed was that he was a little more dandruffy than usual, but that didn't seem like the right thing to say. And then he said, "I shaved!" Which makes it official: I am the last guy in the seventh grade to shave. Well, second-to-last. There's Dan Cramer, but he skipped two grades and is, like, ten, so he doesn't count.

I don't know why it's taking me so long—there are girls in my class with more hair on their faces than me. (Not that I envy them that, either. But still.)

In English today, Mr. Parker had us spend the whole class diagramming sentences at the blackboard. Diagramming sentences is like a combination of the worst parts of doing math with the worst parts of doing English. It's a total waste of time, because you can either speak English or you can't, and if you can't, there's no point in drawing lines all over your sentences. Doug Spivak thinks that *gooder* means the same thing as *better*, and no amount of diagramming sentences will fix that.

I asked Dad at dinner whether there's any job where you have to diagram sentences, and he said, "Teaching middle-school kids English."

JANUARY 11 [mood: annoyed]

Today, Mr. Parker had us diagram sentences again. I told him that I didn't want to have to keep doing this, because the only job where you have to diagram sentences is middle-school teacher, and I plan on doing something better than that. He didn't say anything. He just got very quiet and gave us all a pop quiz on diagramming sentences. I got a D.

Last night, Sophie was watching *Lady and the Tramp*, and I watched a little of it with her. It got to the scene where the Tramp takes Lady to the restaurant, and the owner brings them the plate of spaghetti and meatballs, and sings and plays a song on the accordion for them, and I started to wonder: What's the chef's story? How do you wind up running a restaurant that serves pasta to dogs? Is that his whole business? Or does he only do it as a sideline? Do the dogs pay him somehow? How does he stay in business? Is he mentally ill? And what about the other kitchen workers? Are they just humoring him? The dog stuff is nice—what with the nose-pushing of the meatball and everything—but it seems to me like there's a far more interesting movie going on right behind them.

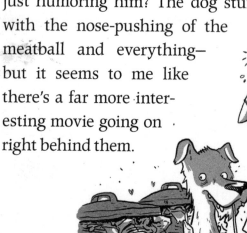

So we've been assigned *Watership Down* in Mr. Parker's English class. We've been reading it for a few weeks now, and during today's class, Doug Spivak raised his hand and said, "Hey, wait a minute: This is about rabbits, isn't it?"

I don't know why this is even surprising. Doug's repeated seventh grade twice, and is the guy who, until he was ten, thought the International House of Pancakes restaurants were actually all made out of pancakes. He's not the sharpest knife in the drawer. In fact, he's more like a spoon or something, sharpness-wise.

My dad's taking fish oil to lower his cholesterol. Whenever I see the bottle, it cracks me up, because I like to imagine it's supposed to be squirted into squeaky fish.

Today in health class, Mrs. Lewis told us that we needed to learn about what it would be like to be a parent. So she paired us off and gave every pair an egg to take care of, like it's a baby and we're its parents. One of us has to keep it with us at all times until Friday, and if it breaks, we get an F for the project. I got paired with Laurie Watson, the co-captain of the field hockey team. It could've been worse—Chuck got paired up with Sam Turner, the defensive tackle for our football team. When Chuck and Sam asked why, Mrs. Lewis said, "Families come in all different configurations. Plus, we have more boys than girls in this class."

After we got our egg, Laurie asked me what we should name the baby. She said she was thinking of maybe naming it Katherine, "but we'll call her Kate or Katie

Baby Katherine

for short." I just stared at her and said, "Laurie, it's an egg." And she said, "Oh, okay. Fine. Be like that. But I'm calling it Katherine." And then she ignored me for the rest of class. I feel like our egg baby is going to have a lot of trouble at home.

Meanwhile, Chuck was fighting with Sam over their egg. Chuck wanted to name it Chuck Jr., while Sam wanted to name it Sam Jr. If they'd asked me, I would've suggested compromising and calling their baby Suck.

It's probably a good thing they didn't ask me.

JANUARY 17 [mood: irritated]

Man. Only a day into parenting this egg, and Laurie and I have already had our first big fight. I took the egg home last night, because Laurie had field hockey practice, and I realized pretty quickly that it was going to be hard to keep the egg from breaking. So I had what I thought was a pretty good idea: I boiled it.

I was kind of proud of myself, but when I gave it back to Laurie before homeroom, she said, "Something doesn't feel right about Katie." So I told her what I'd done, and she said "You boiled our baby?" so loud that everyone in the hallway turned and stared. I pointed out that at least I didn't poach or scramble our baby, but that didn't seem to make things any better.

Later, Laurie came up to me at lunch and said that she was thinking of asking Mrs. Lewis to let her have sole custody of the egg, with me only allowed supervised visits, but then she realized that really wouldn't be much of a punishment for me, and besides, she needed me to look after the egg during her violin lessons.

JANUARY 18 [mood: Jedi-ish]

Is Jabba a common name throughout the *Star Wars* universe? And does each planet have only one of them? Because it seems odd to me that you'd need to go by "Jabba the Hutt." It makes me wonder if he had one too

many phone calls that went like this:

"Hey, it's me, Jabba."

"Jabba the Ewok?"

"No, the other one."

"Jabba the Gungan?"

"No."

"Jabba the Dagoban?"

"No. C'mon, man. It's me, Jabba! Jabba the Hutt!"

"Oh! Jabba the Hutt! Why didn't you say so?"

JANUARY 19 [mood: anxious]

During health class today, Mrs. Lewis announced that, so far, four out of the twelve couples in our class have broken their egg babies. Then she said that any couple who kept their egg intact would get a bonus A for the semester, and Sam got so excited, he accidentally high-fived Chuck with his egg-holding hand, and Sam Jr. went everywhere. Chuck didn't seem too upset about it, though. He said that he and Sam had been fighting a lot about how to take care of the egg, and he was kind of glad to have that over with.

Well, today was the final day for the egg-baby experiment, and I'm really happy, because I was sick of taking care of my stupid egg. In class, when it came time for us to give our eggs back to Mrs. Lewis, Laurie and I were one of only three couples who'd kept their eggs intact all week long, and she said she was very proud of us. Then she leaned on her desk a little, and our egg rolled off and fell on the floor. That's when Mrs. Lewis realized ours had been boiled. She told us she was very, very disappointed in us, and hoped that we didn't have a baby for many, many years. I told her that made two of us.

[mood: hungry] JANUARY 21

Chuck and I were debating: If a fast-food mascot were making your food, which one would you go with—Ronald McDonald, the Burger King, Wendy, or the Arby's hat? We both agreed that we wouldn't choose the hat, but after that, it got harder. I said

I'd go with the King, but Chuck pointed out that a king probably has people preparing food for him, so he'd be unfamiliar with proper cooking techniques and wouldn't know how to cook your food to the proper internal temperature. (Chuck had food poisoning once, and ever since, he's been terrified of it. I once saw him ask a lunch lady to reheat his pudding cup to kill any bacteria.) Chuck said he'd go with Wendy, but I said that she was even less likely to know anything about preventing food poisoning. Plus, I know how gross my little sister, Sophie, is, and I wouldn't trust anything she prepared. So that left Ronald McDonald, and we both agreed that if we had to choose between a burger made by a clown and nothing, we'd pick nothing.

I was hanging out at Chuck's place last night, and his older sister, Tracy, had rented *Twilight: New Moon*, so we watched it with her. I have to give it credit: I never knew a movie about a vampire fighting a were-wolf could be so boring.

Sophie came home from school today all excited because she got cast in the school play as Gretel in *Hansel and Gretel*. She was super super happy, because she'd beaten out Sara Cambert, her big rival. Sophie kept talking about how crushed Sara was. Sara's been in a local furniture commercial and was sure that she was going to be picked for the role, but instead, she's going to have to play a bush, "and not even one of the good bushes." Finally, my mom said, "Well, it's going to be a lot of work. You'll have to learn your lines." And Sophie said, "What lines?" My mom explained that if you're in a play, you have to know what to say and do, so Sophie would have to practice her lines every night instead of watching TV, and my dad said it would be a good lesson in the value of hard work. Then Sophie got super quiet and just kept muttering about how Sara Cambert had "won this round."

JANUARY 24 [mood: excited]

After dinner tonight, my sister said that she'd asked her teacher about learning her lines, and "Mrs. McKenna told me that I should practice them with someone. She said it'd be easy for me to remember my lines if I just spent an hour or two every night with my parents going through the script. It'll be a good lesson in the value of hard work, right?" My dad looked at my mom, and my mom looked at my dad, and then they both looked at me. And my mom said, "Tad, you know how you've been asking for a new skateboard?" And that is how I wound up helping Sophie learn her lines for her play.

Argh. I've been going through the *Hansel and Gretel* script every night with Sophie, and it's really no fun. The whole play's written in rhyme, so all of her lines rhyme with the one that came right before, and she still can't remember them. I'll read Hansel's part and say something like, "Look at that house! It's so fine and so dandy!" and then I'll look at her and she'll just be like, "I don't know." And so I'll give her part of her line: "It looks delicious, like it's made out of . . . ?" And she'll still be like, "What? I don't know. Bricks?"

I hate helping Sophie—it's a big waste of time.
     And the worst part is, I'm now thinking in rhyme.

Just three more days till I get my reward.
This is too much work for a stupid skateboard.

JANUARY 27 [mood:  exhausted]

Well, Sophie's getting a little better at learning her lines. Tonight, for the first time, I said Hansel's line, "Now's your chance, Gretel, start doing some shovin'!" and she said, "Something something something, something something oven?" It's a start.

[mood: relieved] **JANUARY 28**

Sophie's big show is tomorrow, and I'm glad I'm finally done helping her. I think she'll actually do OK—it took a while, but she learned all her lines, more or less. I'm just happy I never have to think about the story of Hansel and Gretel ever again. It's a weird story. Like, why would anyone want to eat a candy house? Wouldn't it be kind of dirty and sticky?

Just got back from Sophie's big play. It was a little ... weird. We got there, and Mrs. McKenna was all panicked, and told my parents the show might not happen because Jerry Moynihan, who played Hansel, was out sick with the stomach flu. And then Sophie said, "My brother, Tad, knows all the lines! He learned them all when he was helping me!" And Mrs. McKenna said, "Oh, that's wonderful! If Tad can play Hansel, the show can go on!" And Mrs. McKenna and Sophie and my parents and all the other kids were looking at me, and just before I could say, "No way," my mom leaned over and whispered in my ear, "*Lord of the Rings* trilogy DVD boxed set." And I said, "Extended versions?" And she said, "Sure."

So at the age of twelve, I just

starred in an elementary-school production of *Hansel and Gretel*. It was fun right up until the moment I noticed Bill Gilbert in the audience—he's in my class, and I guess his younger brother's in Sophie's class. I think I'd better get ready to be called Hansel at school for the next month or so.

Still, it was pretty nice to help Sophie out. She seemed really happy afterward. I asked her why, and she said, "Did you see how sad Sara Cambert looked in her bush costume?" And then she just laughed and kept imitating her, going "I'm Sara Cambert! I'm a bush! I only have one line!"

Sophie scares me sometimes.

JANUARY 30 [mood: amused]

We have a new exchange student in our class— Claudine Moreau from France. I felt kind of bad for her, because in social studies, Mrs. Wexler said, "Well, class, I think it's exciting to have someone from another country here! Would anyone like to ask Claudine anything about France?" And everyone just kind of sat there feeling embarrassed for her, until Doug Spivak raised his hand and said,

"What do your toasters look like?" And Mrs. Wexler said, "Why would you ask that, of all things?" And Doug said, "Well, I've always wondered how the French make French toast. Like, do you pour the egg and milk into the toaster, or what? It seems messy and dangerous." And Mrs. Wexler said, "Does anyone *else* have anything to ask?"

After class, I saw Doug asking Claudine about French onions, and whether they come out of the ground covered in melted cheese. She looked really confused.

JANUARY 31 [mood: nauseated]

I think the most upsetting nursery rhyme has to be "Pop Goes the Weasel," what with the whole exploding-weasel thing.

Wait, exploding what?!

February

I would be writing this on the computer in the family room, but Sophie's in there right now, watching reruns of *Hannah Montana.* I still can't believe there's a show where the whole plot is that nobody can tell that Hannah Montana is Miley Cyrus in a wig. The kids in

I mean, come on, guys, really?!

her school make Clark Kent's coworkers look like brain surgeons.

The only way that show would make sense would be if there were a title card at the beginning of every episode that said, "Everyone in this town has had the exact same kind of brain injury that destroys your ability to recognize things, even if those things look exactly alike."

FEBRUARY 2 [mood: groundhoggy]

This morning in homeroom, Mrs. Coleman wished us all a happy Groundhog Day. Then our exchange student, Claudine Moreau, raised her hand and asked, "What is a groundhog day?" So Mrs. Coleman tried to explain it to her, and Claudine asked a lot of questions, like, "How does anyone know if the groundhog actually sees its shadow or not?" But finally, she said she understood: "You Americans believe a rodent controls the weather. In France, we have—how you say?—meteorologists?"

When she put it like that, it did sound kind of stupid.

Went to the mall with my parents today. Sophie and I stopped by the pet store, which is sort of like going to a crappy, free zoo. They had a whole litter of Dalmatian puppies there, and they were pretty cute. Although seeing Dalmatian puppies up close, I didn't understand why Cruella De Vil thought she needed 101 of them to make a coat. I feel like you could make a really nice coat with six or seven of them. Which, it turns out, isn't the sort of thing you're supposed to say out loud in a pet store, because the clerk kind of asked us to leave.

FEBRUARY 5 [mood: picky]

Werewolves are badly named. They're not people who *were* wolves. They're people who *are* wolves. They should be called arewolves. (Or, if you're going to be super accurate, aresometimeswolves.)

[mood: hopeful] FEBRUARY 6

At school today, the signs went up for the after-school Valentine's Day dance. I really want to ask Katie Zembla from my geometry class.

She seems super friendly and pretty, and she's always really nice to me after I let her copy my homework.

FEBRUARY 7 [mood: still hopeful]

I tried asking Katie to the dance today, but I got all nervous and wound up asking to borrow her eraser instead. And then I had to erase some stuff so it wouldn't look weird, which meant that I wound up erasing a couple of answers on my homework right before I had to hand it in.

[mood: still hopeful] FEBRUARY 8

I tried asking Katie again, but I wound up asking to borrow her protractor. It's getting embarrassing.

FEBRUARY 9 [mood: very happy]

Good news! I finally asked her, and she said she'd go with me! Well, actually, she said she'd go if this person she's waiting to ask her doesn't by tomorrow. So I'm her second choice!

It's Friday, and I caught up with Katie after class. She said her first choice still hadn't asked her, but she wanted to give him until the end of the day, so she said she'd call me tomorrow.

Hooray! I just called Katie, and she said she'd go with me! The dance is three days away, so I have until then to find out stuff like what to wear and how to dance.

Mom took me to the mall today to look for a new tie. I like the one I have, but she says girls don't like boys who wear ties that look like fish.

Tomorrow's the big dance! I went to the Dollar Depot today and bought some cK One cologne. Well, actually, it's called dB Two, but it smells just like cK One, and it only costs a buck! It's pretty good—my dad noticed it right when he came home, and I was all the way up in my room. He asked how much I paid for it, and when I told him, he said, "That's a bargain for cologne that strong!" And then he opened all the windows.

Ugh. I didn't wind up going to the dance after all. I woke up this morning covered in hives.

Mom took me to Dr. Bauer, who tested me and told me that I'm allergic to the artificial musk in the dB Two, which I guess is good to know. He gave me some Benadryl, and I spent the day at home, recovering. So instead of going to the dance, I stayed home and watched TV with my parents. They tried to be nice about it, but every once in a while, my dad would look at me and start laughing, and then he'd try to pretend that he was laughing at the TV, but we were watching reruns of *Law & Order: SVU*, which isn't really all that funny.

FEBRUARY 15 [mood:  ill]

At the grocery store tonight, they were giving away boxes of those Valentine's candy hearts for free because, as the cashier said, "It's not like any-one's going to buy them the day after Valentine's Day." I just ate a few of them and then threw them away. Valentine's hearts are the worst candy on earth. They're, like, made of sugar, soap, and chalk dust.

The family went out to dinner tonight to Chili's, and in the restroom, they had this sign:

It made me wonder if any customer has ever wound up just standing there in front of the sink, waiting for an employee to come wash his hands for him.

NOTICE
EMPLOYEES MUST WASH HANDS

[mood: excited] **FEBRUARY 20**

So I just got back from brushing my teeth, and when I was done, I noticed something: I've got a little bit of hair growing in on my upper lip. At first I thought it was a shadow, but I looked closer and it's definitely a mustache. I may finally be ready to start shaving. I considered asking my parents to get me a razor, but then I decided that I'd let it go for a while and see how long it takes for anyone to notice.

FEBRUARY 21 [mood: mature]

Today was the first day for my new mustache. There's something about having a mustache that makes you feel automatically more mature. I spent the whole day feeling like Johnny Depp in *Pirates of the Caribbean*—holding doors for girls and trying to come up with clever, Jack Sparrow-y things to say to them. When Julie Underhill asked me in class today if she could borrow a pen, I said, "You can borrow anything you like." And she said, "Oh. Um. Well, can I borrow a pen?" And then I realized that I didn't have any pens to loan her. But still—it sounded really cool.

I'm kind of surprised my parents haven't noticed my mustache yet. I feel like it's pretty noticeable— it's the only thing I can see when I look in the mirror. At dinner tonight, whenever my parents asked me anything, I'd pause and think about it while stroking my mustache with my thumb and forefinger. But after I did that when Sophie asked me to pass the turnips, my mom said, "Are you feeling OK? Are you sick? Come over here!" and took my temperature by pressing her lips to my forehead, which I don't think is the sort of thing you do to someone who has a mustache.

[mood: embarrassed] FEBRUARY 23

So today at school, Señora Lutz asked me why I was late to Spanish class, and I said, "Wouldn't you like to know?" And she said, "Yes I would. And I'd appreciate it if you didn't take that tone with me." Maybe the light was too low in the room for her to see my mustache. After class, Chuck said, "Why've you been talking weird lately?" And I said, "I can't imagine what you're talking about." And he said, "You've got, like, this weird British accent all of a sudden. You sound like a drunk Mary Poppins."

Well, today, I got tired of waiting for my parents to mention my mustache. So when my mom said she was going to the store and asked if I needed anything, I just said, "Maybe some razors?" And she said, "Why?" And I said, "Isn't it obvious?" And she said, "No. Not really." And I said, "My mustache!" And then she walked over and looked at my face really closely and said, "Eh. I don't see it."

Since my mom wouldn't get me any razors, I decided to shave using one of my dad's disposable razors this morning. I couldn't find any shaving cream, so I used some of my mom's hairstyling foam. It turns out that styling foam is super sticky, and razors are a lot sharper than you'd expect. So I came down to breakfast with a Band-Aid across my upper lip and another one on my chin. (I wasn't even growing any hair there, but I figured it'd be good to practice shaving my whole face.)

My dad saw me and said, "Whoa! Tad—what happened to your fa—" But then my mom kicked him under the table and he quieted down. Neither of them said anything about it for the rest of the day, but just now, when I came upstairs to the bathroom to brush my teeth, there was a new electric razor there. I can't wait to use it the next time my mustache grows in. Hopefully, by then my face scars will have healed. And if anyone at school asks, I'm telling them I got into a fight.

From boy...

...to man!

I never understand why *Jeopardy!* does that whole weird "You have to phrase your answers in the form of a question" thing. But I think I've figured out a loophole: If I ever wind up on *Jeopardy!*, I'll buzz in every time and ask the question, "What is an answer in this episode of *Jeopardy!*?" And they'd have to let me win, because that is technically right.

I can't believe nobody else has thought of this.

Today in science, we learned that monkeys and apes are different species: Monkeys have tails, while apes don't. So a marmoset, for instance, is a monkey, while a chimpanzee is an ape.

Doug Spivak raised his hand and asked, "What if you cut the tail off a marmoset? Does it become an ape? And what if you attach that tail to a chimpanzee? Does it become a monkey?" We never found out the answer, because Mr. Parker just put his head down on his desk and made a noise like he was either laughing or crying—it was hard to tell.

Today's Leap Day—the day that comes only once every four years. I feel like whoever came up with Leap Day should go down to the hospital and apologize to all the babies that were born today, because thanks to that person, they're in for a long life of explaining their birthday to people.

March

Overslept this morning and missed the school bus, so my mom had to drive me to school. I blame my alarm clock. Why do they even put a Snooze button on there? They might as well just call it an Oversleep button.

In my science textbook, I read that even blind chameleons change color to match their surroundings.

I asked my dad how they figured that out, and he said, "Well, I guess they did a study where they blinded some chameleons and then saw what happened."

I think it's weird that somewhere out there in the world, there's a guy whose job title is Chameleon Blinder.

MARCH 3 [mood: thoughtful]

I've been thinking about it, and if I ever have a band, it will be called Chameleon Blinder.

Getting a little excited for my birthday—it's in three days. I'm not having a big party or anything—my parents are going to take Chuck and Kevin and Jake bowling with me, and then out for pizza at Pizza Land.

I told my mom I want a GamePort XL game system for my birthday. Chuck got one for Christmas, and he brought it to school last week. He let me see it. That's all he let me do, though—see it. He wouldn't let me hold it because, he said, "My mom said I can't let people play with it, because they might break it. Plus, it's flu season, so it's better not to touch things other people have touched." (Chuck's a nice guy, but his mom's super nervous about everything, and as a result, so's he. Until he was in sixth grade, his mom made Chuck wear a helmet on the school bus.)

The GamePort XL is pretty cool—there's a game that makes it look like it's got a puppy inside it, and you can make it fetch and stay and stuff. Chuck really likes it because his mom won't let him have a dog, because she's afraid it might one day go crazy and kill him just like this dog she saw on the news. I told Chuck that if I get that game, I'm naming my puppy "Chuckbiter."

I really need a GamePort XL. In study hall today, Chuck and Kevin both spent the whole time playing with their imaginary dogs.

I had nothing to do but draw pictures of blind chameleons:

At breakfast, I reminded my mom and dad that I want a GamePort XL for my birthday, and my mom said, "Well, maybe if you're good, you'll get that GigaPet 9000 you want." And I got all worried and said, "No! I want a GamePort XL! Why did you think I wanted a GigaPet? Those are for seven-year-old girls!" And she said, "Oh, a GamePort? Well, it's probably too late to get you one of those." And then she smiled at my dad. So I think they're just messing with my head. Which isn't very nice.

Awesome!

Not awesome!

Today was my birthday. Bowling and dinner were a lot of fun. (Well, there were two bad parts: First, even though I told him not to do it, my dad told the people at Pizza Land that it was my birthday, so all the waiters and the Pizza Badger came over and sang "Happy Birthday" to me, which would've been fun when I was, like, nine, but I'm thirteen now. And then the fact that I was being serenaded by the Pizza Badger made Kevin laugh so loud, he sprayed soda through his nose and onto my cake. We had to eat around that part.)

Hey, hey, HEY! Party dudes!

Let's pizza PARTY!

When we got home, my parents gave me my present: a Game-Port XL! So I can't blog now–I'm teaching Chuckbiter to fetch.

Bad news. I went over to Chuck's today, and Kevin came over, and we were all playing with our

GamePorts. And then I put mine on the floor and went to the kitchen to get a soda, and then, when I came back, I stepped on it and broke it.

I don't even know what was worse—breaking my GamePort or having Chuck's mom come in the room immediately afterward and say, "You see, Chuck? That's why you shouldn't let Tad touch your things."

I bet that if all the animal mascots for products got together for a convention—like, if the Trix rabbit and the Cocoa Puffs cuckoo and Elsie the cow all got together—I kind of think that everyone would make a point of avoiding the Charmin toilet-paper bears. Seriously. As best I can tell, those bears would talk about nothing but toilet paper, and everyone else would be like, "Hey, we're trying to eat over here."

For vocab in English, we have to learn the word *disgruntled*. It means "unhappy." Weirdly, there's no such word as *gruntled*, meaning "happy." I'm going to try and make it a word, though. I'm just going to start using it in conversation, and hopefully it'll catch on.

Well, after one day, I'm giving up on making *gruntled* a word. I told my mom that I was gruntled with dinner last night, and she said if I didn't like it, I didn't have to eat it. I told Mr. Parker today that I was feeling gruntled, and he said, "If you need to go to the bathroom, just ask to be excused." And then I told one of the lunch ladies today that the food was very gruntling, and she said she'd had enough abuse from us kids.

Making words catch on is a lot harder than I'd thought. It gave me a whole new respect for Merriam and Webster.

Today at school, we all pretty much wasted a whole period of social studies. Mrs. Wexler was explaining how the United States engages in trade with other countries, like Mexico and Canada. Doug Spivak raised his hand and said, "I'm sorry, Mrs. Wexler? But Canada's a state." And Mrs. Wexler said, "No, Doug, actually, Canada is a whole separate country." But Doug said, "No, it's a state. States have their names on quarters, right?" And then he reached into his pocket and held up a quarter and said, "I got this Canadian quarter a little while ago, and it says 'Canada' on it. So they must be a state. A state full of stupid people who don't know how to make quarters that work in vending machines."

So then Mrs. Wexler spent a while explaining that while Canada uses dollars and quarters, that doesn't make them a state. And Doug said, "But they speak English! That means they must be American!" And she said, "Just because they speak English somewhere doesn't mean it's part of America. I mean, Great Britain's not part of America, is it?" And he said, "It's not?" And things went on like that for another half hour.

I bet Doug Spivak's going to get held back again this year. It's too bad. He kind of makes every class more interesting.

MARCH 17   [mood: green]

Today is St. Patrick's Day. Supposedly, St. Patrick's the guy who got all the snakes out of Ireland. I dunno—that doesn't seem like a sainthood-worthy achievement. I mean, committing reptile genocide is really hard to do, but it doesn't seem like it makes you a saint so much as it makes you a really, really good exterminator.

MARCH 18 [mood: bored]

Sophie and I played Monopoly tonight. I'm not sure how that game ever got made. Like, did someone go into Parker Brothers and say, "I have an idea for a game: A dog, a flat iron, a shoe, and a hat are all buying streets. Sometimes, one of them will go to jail for no good reason. Plus, there's an old man with a bag full of money who sometimes wins beauty pageants, there are some railroads, and it never ends and there's no way to tell who won."

It's like a board game based on someone's nightmare.

[mood: excited] MARCH 19

Today in science class, Mr. Parker said that any-one who enters the science fair this year will get extra credit—and whoever wins will get an A for the semester. I went home and looked on the inter-net for science fair project ideas, and I found one that looks unbeatable: You can make a volcano out of clay, and put baking soda, vinegar, and red food coloring inside it to make "lava" flow out of it. I don't know what the big science lesson is supposed to be from that, because I'm pretty sure that's not how real volcanoes work.

Then again, I don't really care what the lesson's supposed to be. I just like the idea of making something that explodes.

MARCH 20 [mood: competitive]

So I asked Chuck today if he was making a science fair project, and he said that he was. And I asked him what it was, and he said he was keeping it a secret, because his was so awesome, he didn't want anyone to steal it. Then he asked me what I was making, and I told him that I wasn't going to tell him, but that it was even awesomer than his. So we made a bet. Whichever one of us wins the science fair will pay the other one ten bucks. I'm already making plans on what to do with my winnings. Like maybe getting a shirt that says "I Won Ten Bucks from Chuck."

Here are some things I learned today while doing my science project:

- If you're going to make a volcano, don't make it out of your sister's old Play-Doh on your kitchen table. Because if you do, when you pour baking soda and vinegar in it, it might start to leak all over the kitchen floor.
- Also, don't use a whole bottle of red food coloring, because the giant puddle on your floor will be super red.
- Also, don't run when you're getting the paper towels to clean up the table and the floor, because you'll just slip and fall and get it all over you.
- Also, try not to time the whole thing to the moment your mom comes home from work. Because it turns out that if your mom walks in the door and finds you under the kitchen table, in the middle of a giant

red puddle, and covered with red liquid,
she'll scream really, really loud, in a way
that you've never heard her scream before.

That is what I have learned about volcanoes
so far.

MARCH 22 [mood: hopeful]

At lunch today, Susan Meyers asked me if I was
doing a science fair project. I told her I was, but
that it was top secret. She said, "Oh, I'm doing one
on optimizing the uses of activated charcoal in a
water-filtration system."

I'm not even sure what that means, but I know
this much: It's no match for a tiny volcano. I'm *so*
going to win.

[mood: bored] **MARCH 23**

In order to do some research on volcanoes, I went
to the library and got a whole bunch of books on
them. I also rented the movies *Volcano* and *Dante's*

Peak. Applying the scientific method, I now have a hypothesis that all movies about volcanoes suck.

MARCH 24   [mood: nervous]

Well, I got the volcano done in time for tomorrow's science fair. I think it looks OK, even though I kind of screwed up in painting it—it was supposed to look gray, but when I put the paint on the clay, it wound up looking dark brown. Sophie kept saying it looks like "a pile of poop," and then laughing, until my mom told her to stop.

I also made a posterboard display covered with facts about volcanoes. For instance, did you know that "Volcano" is the nickname for rugby player Lesley Vainikolo? Wikipedia is awesome.

You know, SCIENCE!

Tonight was the school science fair. My parents helped me bring my volcano in and set it up. Then Chuck got there with his parents and his science project: a volcano that erupts baking soda and vinegar. And then other kids started coming in, and it turns out that, like, twelve guys from my class all made volcanoes. I guess we all went to the same website and got the same idea. Three other kids even had pictures of Lesley Vainikolo as part of their displays. Stupid Wikipedia.

So I'm not getting an A in science after all. In fact, Mr. Parker seemed so unimpressed that by the time he got to me, he said, "Don't even bother pouring the vinegar in. I get it. It's a volcano."

Susan Meyers won the science fair. I was pretty sad about it, until Mr. Parker told her that she'd have to compete in the regional science fair, which takes place during our spring vacation. Chuck and I agreed: We were glad we hadn't won.

Afterward, I took my volcano over to Chuck's house and we put some of his little brother's Lego men in front of both of them, poured vinegar in them, and videotaped the whole thing. It was sort of like *Dante's Peak* meets *Volcano,* but with better acting.

MARCH 26 [mood: hungry]

I've never understood why it's such a big deal in *Green Eggs and Ham* that Sam won't eat green eggs and ham. Not eating green eggs and ham seems like a really good policy to me.

[mood: denial] **MARCH 29**

Oh, man. So I came down to breakfast this morning, and my mom looked really sad, and my dad said: "Your great-aunt Sophie died yesterday." And I said, "Which one was she?" And my dad said, "She was your mother's father's sister." And I said, "The one with the bright-red hair?" And my mom said, "No. That's your great-aunt Katie. Sophie's the one with the cane." And I said, "Oh! You mean the mean one who always picked her terrier up by the neck? Wasn't she dead already?" And my dad gave me a look that told me that was the wrong thing to say.

Great-Aunt Sophie (R.I.P.)   Great-Aunt Katie (not dead)

My little sister Sophie's pretty upset—she was named for our great-aunt Sophie. She came into my room tonight and said, "Where do you think Aunt Sophie went?" And I gave her the same answer my parents gave me when our golden retriever died: Great-Aunt Sophie was taken to a farm where she gets to spend all day chasing rabbits and playing with other great-aunts.

That seemed to make her happy.

MARCH 30   [mood: slightly irregular]

After school today, Mom took me to the outlet mall to buy a new suit for Great-Aunt Sophie's funeral, because I outgrew my last one. Mom always takes me to the outlet mall to get clothes. One day, when I'm older, I want to wear clothes with labels that don't have the words SLIGHTLY IRREGULAR stamped on them. I wanted to get a suit with big pinstripes, like Jay-Z would wear, but Mom wouldn't let me—she made me get a really boring black one instead. When I got it home and showed my dad, he said, "Are you leaning over to your left?" And I said, "No." That's when we realized that the right arm was a lot shorter than the left one. Stupid irregular suit. Now I'm going to have to spend all day Saturday leaning slightly to the right, to compensate.

MARCH 31 [mood: relieved]

Well, today was the funeral. Everyone said nice things about Great-Aunt Sophie, but the truth is, she smoked nonstop and hit her terrier with her cane and was super mean. She wasn't a nice lady. But I guess you can't say that at a funeral. So everyone pretended to be really sad. Except for her terrier. He looked happier than I'd ever seen him.

April

Attention, friends of Tad!

If you go onto Facebook and find <u>this profile</u> with my name on it, please be aware that IT IS NOT my profile! It is a fake profile that my friend Chuck put up as a stupid April Fools'

facebook

Name: Tad
Age: 12
Interests: nose-picking, butt-scratching, playing classical banjo, and dressing up like a girl.

joke. He thought it would be funny. But if I had a Facebook profile, I wouldn't list my interests as "nose-picking, butt-scratching, playing classical banjo, and dressing up like a girl." I don't even like the banjo.

However, rest assured that <u>this profile</u> of Chuck is the real one. Honestly, I'm as surprised as anyone to find out that Chuck cried at the end of *Titanic* and still wets the bed, but if that's what his profile says, then it must be true.

APRIL 2 [mood: annoyed]

When I was at Great-Aunt Sophie's funeral, I saw my uncle Scott, and he taught me a new joke. When he saw me, he said, "Hey, how've you been? Do you want a henway?" And I said, "What's a henway?" And he said, "Oh, about three pounds."

Get it? Because it sounds like I was asking, "What's a hen weigh?"

So I tried telling the joke today. First I tried it on Chuck—he asked how my trip to Great-Aunt Sophie's funeral was, and I said, "It was good, except I lost my henway." And he said, "A henway?

I don't know what a henway is." Then I tried it on Señora Lutz, when she asked where my Spanish book was, and I said, "I must've left it in my locker next to my henway," and she just sighed and said, "Well, run back and get it." Finally I tried it on Doug Spivak in social studies—I asked him if he'd remembered to bring his henway. And he said, "What's a henway?" And I said, "Oh, about three pounds." And he thought about it for a few seconds, and then he said, "I don't get it."

I don't care. I still think it's an awesome joke.

APRIL 3 [mood: excited]

Hooray! I've been practicing for weeks, and I finally figured out how to do a kickflip on my skateboard! Well, sort of—I can jump up and flip the skateboard beneath me, but I haven't figured out how to actually land on anything other than my face. Still, though, the first half looks pretty great. And besides, landing isn't important. The important thing is, I can take a picture of me in midair and put it on my Facebook page, and it'll look awesome.

Gaaaargh! Chuck and I spent all afternoon in his driveway, trying to get a picture of me doing my kickflip, but my dad's digital camera really sucks. Here are some of the photos we took:

This one was taken, like, a second too soon.

This one was taken a second too late.

This one is of Chuck's finger. He's not a very good photographer.

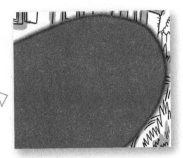

Anyway. We're going to try again next weekend.

Hopefully, by then the swelling in my face will have gone down.

Easter Sunday's in a few days, and Sophie's been talking a lot about the Easter Bunny lately. All through dinner, she kept saying stuff like, "I hope the Easter bunny brings me lots of Cadbury Creme Eggs!" or "Does the Easter Bunny know I don't like licorice jelly beans?" I asked her how the Easter Bunny makes Peeps, and she explained about the Easter Bunny's Peep factory, and my parents just sort of nudged each other and smiled.

What they don't know is that back when she was six, Sophie told me that she'd figured out that the Easter Bunny doesn't exist. But she'd also figured out that Mom and Dad really like pretending to be the Easter Bunny, and that they probably give her more candy than they would if they knew that she knew that they were the ones leaving it. And since they have to give me the same amount of stuff they give Sophie, I've realized that it's in my best interest to keep my parents believing in Sophie's belief in the Easter Bunny. So we both put on this little show for my parents. It's actually sort of cute how excited they get about it. I mean, I know that it can't go on forever, but it's sort of fun while it lasts.

APRIL 6 [mood:  happy]

Good news! I was talking to Chuck and Kevin today, and Chuck mentioned how we're trying to take the skateboard picture. It turns out, Kevin's dad has a really nice high-speed digital camera that's amazing at taking action shots. Kevin said he could sneak it out and let us borrow it, but that we'd have to be super careful, 'cause it's a nice camera and really expensive. And then he mentioned it again. And then he mentioned it a third time.

Kevin worries a lot.

[mood: hungry] **APRIL 7**

Tonight at the grocery store, my mom sent me off to buy Easter candy while she distracted Sophie.

I bought a bunch of chocolate stuff and some Peeps. Did you know that the official name of Peeps is "Marshmallow Peeps"?

MEAT

MARSHMALLOW

Peeps

Why would you bother putting the word *Marshmallow* on there? It's not like there are other kinds of Peeps, and you have to call them Marshmallow Peeps to prevent people from confusing them with Cheese Peeps or Meat Peeps.

APRIL 8 [mood: hyper]

Well, today was Easter, so I woke up to the sound of Sophie running around the living room screaming at the top of her lungs. I came downstairs and found out that she'd already eaten the ears off her chocolate rabbit, a Cadbury Creme Egg, and a whole box of Peeps, and my mom had taken her Easter basket away from her. Sophie really can't handle her candy.

Then we had breakfast, and my mom told the same story she tells every year, about how when I was five, we went to a petting zoo on Easter to see the rabbits, and my parents told me, "Look! It's the Easter Bunny!" and I ate some of what I thought were tiny chocolate eggs that the Easter Bunny had laid. Sophie loves hearing that story, but I still don't see what's so funny about it.

[mood: scared]

Ohhhhhh crap. Kevin gave me his dad's camera today, and I put it in my backpack. But when I got home, I kind of forgot the camera was in there, so I

did what I usually do with my backpack, which is
throw it into the corner of my room. That's when I
heard a noise. A bad noise, like someone else's dad's
camera breaking. And sure enough, when I took it
out and turned it on,
the camera just made
this weird whining
noise.

Oh crap oh crap oh
crap.

Oh crap.

I took Kevin's dad's camera to the camera store
today, to ask about how to fix it. I was sort of hop-
ing they'd tell me that it just, like, needed a new
battery or something. But instead, the creepy guy
at the camera store who looks sort of like Elmer
Fudd told me that I'd knocked the lens out of
alignment. I asked him what that means, and he
told me it means that I need to pay him $300. I
told him I'd just try and fix it myself, then. That's
when he told me that just having had him look at

the camera would cost me $50. I told him I didn't have $50. He said he'd keep the camera until I did.

Great. All I wanted was a picture of me doing my kickflip. Now Kevin's dad's camera is broken and being held for ransom by Elmer Fudd.

$50 or the camera gets it!

APRIL 11   [mood: depressed]

I did some looking on the internet. It turns out you really can't repair a digital camera by yourself. So I need $350.

I gathered together all my money today, and went through all the sofa cushions in the house, twice. You know, just in case someone had dropped 1,400 quarters in there lately. Nobody had. In total, I have $37. That's $313 less than I need. I'm too embarrassed to ask my mom and dad, which means I need to figure out a way to get that much money, and fast. There is one option, but it's too scary to even think about.

I tried to avoid Kevin all day at school today, but he cornered me at lunch and asked me where his dad's camera was. I lied and told him I'd left it at home. He said to be sure to bring it in tomorrow, because his dad was looking for it.

So I had no choice: I borrowed money from Sophie. She's kept every penny anyone ever gave her—all her allowances and birthday checks and even her money from the Tooth Fairy. I asked

if I could borrow the money, and pay her back with my summer job money. She told me she'd loan me the $313, but only if I paid her back $375 in three months. Also, she told me that I might owe even more money, if something called the "prime lending rate" goes up.

Sophie is the scariest seven-year-old in the universe.

So I went to the store, and Elmer Fudd fixed the camera. I paid him the money and went to Kevin's house and gave him the camera. I don't know how I'm going to pay back Sophie, but at least everything's over.

[mood: depressed]

So Kevin came up to me at lunch today and said, "Hey, what did you do to my dad's camera?" I almost puked up my ravioli, but instead I just said, "Nothing. I didn't do anything." Then he said, "Are you sure?" And I said, "Yeah." And that's when he told me that the weirdest thing had happened. His dad told him he'd dropped the camera a few weeks ago, and it had stopped working. That's why he'd been looking for it—to take it in for repairs—but now it was working fine again. Kevin shrugged and said, "Funny, huh?"

Yeah. It's funny. It's frickin' hilarious.

[mood: thoughtful]

APRIL 14

If the Mario Brothers were real people, I bet Luigi would constantly be wondering, "Just once, why can't we be referred to as the Luigi Brothers?"

APRIL 15 [mood: puzzled]

Do Chinese people have Scrabble?

[mood: nauseous] APRIL 16

Today in social studies class, we learned about the Donner Party, which is nowhere near as much fun as the word *party* makes it sound. They were a group of pioneers who were going across the country and ran out of food, so they wound up eating each other. I think there was more to the story, but I spent the rest of the period distracted by trying to figure out how that worked—like, did they cook the people they ate? Or eat them raw? How did they decide who'd get eaten and who'd be doing the eating? Did they just start with the fat guys? Or what?

I looked through my textbook for more information, but they didn't have anything—not even a recipe. I hate textbooks. They always leave out the most important parts.

I also think that the Donner Party's situation would have made for the best episode ever of *Little House on the Prairie*.

So in all my classes, we're getting ready for the statewide standardized tests we have to take at the end of the month. Anyone who scores above a 90% on an exam will automatically get an A in that subject for the semester.

Today in social studies, Mrs. Wexler made us all take practice evaluation tests, so we'll be used to them by the time we have to take the real ones. It took a while, though, because every time she started to say that we needed to use a number two pencil, Doug Spivak laughed uncontrollably about the words *number two*.

[mood: embarrassed]   **APRIL 18**

Today was a very bad day. My math teacher, Ms. Bolton, came in with a Band-Aid on her cheek, and Chuck passed me a note that said, "What's with the Band-Aid?" And I wrote a note back that said, "I don't know. Maybe she cut herself shaving?" But as I passed it to him, Wendy Gilman (who's been mad at Chuck ever since he accidentally gave her a bloody nose in a kickball game) grabbed it and raised her hand and said, "Ms. Bolton! Tad and Chuck were passing this note!" So Ms. Bolton took it and read it, and then she got really quiet, and

her mustache got a little quivery, and then she said that she was done teaching our class for the day and we should quietly read our math books for the rest of the period.

I think it would probably be a really good idea if Chuck and I did well on the standardized test, because I don't think we're getting good grades in math this semester.

Ms. Bolton

APRIL 19   [mood: terrified]

Ms. Bolton gave everyone an oral pop quiz today. She asked most people what 2 plus 3 is, or what the square root of 9 is. She asked Chuck to explain the proof of Fermat's Last Theorem. She asked me for *pi* to 25 digits.

Yep. We're in trouble.

Ugh. I spent last night working on practice problems, trying to get ready for the math exam. On the plus side, if I ever find myself on a train heading east at 90 miles an hour, and learn that there's a train 500 miles away, heading directly toward me at 75 miles an hour, I'll know exactly how much time I have left to live. So that's nice.

I wonder how it is that the X-Men all got their names. Like, did they get to pick their own? I'm sure that Storm wasn't named "Storm" by her parents, and, coincidentally, wound up being able to control the weather. I bet there was some time for all of them where they tried out different names to see if they would fit. Like, for a couple of weeks, Cyclops had everyone calling him "Bright Eyes," and Wolverine went around practicing signing his name as "Slicey-Hands," just to see if that seemed like a good fit for him.

APRIL 22 [mood: bored]

I think a better show than *Deal or No Deal* would be *Deal, No Deal, or Eels*, where one of the briefcases is full of angry eels.

If sphere *n* has a radius of 2 inches and is placed within cube *z*, which measures 4 inches on each side, who will care?

    A) Tad

    B) None of the above

    (Answer: B)

Here's what I wonder about the Legend of Zelda: Every time they come out with a new game, it's all about how Zelda got kidnapped again, or frozen, or sent back in time, or whatever. And I'm beginning to think that, at a certain point, she should rescue her own dang self. It's not like I don't enjoy the games. It's just that I think that there should be a button you can push so that, when you reach the end of a game and she's thanking you, you can go, "What's your problem? Seriously—getting kidnapped once or twice, I can understand. But I'm beginning to think you just like having people rescue you."

Well, today was the big math exam. I don't want to get my hopes up, but I think I did really well. (If nothing else, I did better than Doug Spivak, who got really angry when he found out that, while it was multiple-choice format, the test wasn't like *Who Wants to Be a Millionaire*, and he wouldn't be allowed to phone a friend on any questions.) After the exam, I talked to Todd Ross, who's the biggest math geek in our class, and he and I had the same answers for almost everything. So I think I might actually do okay this semester. Which is good, 'cause I can't wait to forget all the stupid math I just had to learn.

APRIL 26 [mood: pledge-y]

This morning in homeroom, while pledging allegiance to the flag, I had an awesome idea for a horror movie: What if a flag became possessed with the soul of a serial killer? And then all these kids pledged allegiance to it, so they had to do whatever the flag told them to do? It'd be sort of like *Children of the Corn*, only with a flag. It would be called *Pledge of Darkness*.

OK, now that I've written it out, it looks sort of stupid. But I swear, it seemed like a really good idea this morning.

I've been thinking more about the pledge. I think a really good prank a country could pull on America would be changing its name to Forwichistan, because then it'd sound like kids were saying, "I pledge allegiance to the flag of the United States of America, and to the republic Forwichistan." If I were the president of, like, Luxembourg, I'd totally do that.

[mood: incredibly depressed] **APRIL 30**

My results from the standardized tests came back today. The good news is, I did OK in most subjects. The bad news is, I got only 18% of the questions right on the math test. Ms. Bolton gave us back our answer sheets, so we could check them against the actual answers and figure out what we did wrong. And that's when I saw that I'd accidentally started filling in ovals on the second question, so all my answers were off by one.

And if that weren't bad enough, Ms. Bolton

announced to the class that everyone did OK on the tests, except for one student, who finished in the "dull-normal range," who did "worse than a monkey filling out the form randomly," and who

was, according to the exam, "brain damaged." And then she stared right at me.

After class, Doug Spivak came up to me and said, "Don't feel so bad, man. 'Dull-normal' is still half-normal, right?" It was nice of him to try and make me feel better. But I wish he hadn't.

May

Sophie's reading *The House at Pooh Corner* right now. I liked those books when I was a kid, even though it bothered me that they never explained what two kangaroos were doing in the middle of England. Did they escape from a zoo? Are they runaway circus animals? I always sort of wished there was a whole book just about how Kanga and Roo got to the Hundred Acre Wood.

OK, this is weird. After math today, I came back to my locker and found this note had been stuck in it:

I have a secret admirer! Which is kind of cool, and kind of creepy. I don't know who it could be. I showed it to Kevin and Chuck. Kevin wants to be a forensic investigator like on *CSI*, and he suggested that we put it under a black light or dust it for fingerprints. But I don't have a black light, or fingerprint dust. (We tried rubbing regular dust on it, but it just got all smudgy.) Then Kevin said it was too bad the note wasn't written in blood, 'cause then we could do a DNA match. I pointed out that we don't have a DNA-matching machine, either. Also, as Chuck said, it's probably a good thing that my secret admirer doesn't write her notes to me in blood.

Today I found another note stuck in my locker:

I showed it to Kevin. He asked if he could see the first note, and he looked at them side by side for a while, then said, "I think it's definitely from the same person who sent you the first note."

Kevin can be a little slow sometimes.

At lunch today, Kevin actually had a good idea: He'd brought in last year's yearbook, and we went through our class and crossed out every girl who'd ever told me she didn't like me, or that I was grossing her out, or to stop talking to her. That got rid of a lot of them. Then we crossed out every girl who already was dating somebody, which got rid of a lot more. And Chuck pointed out that we could also cross off every girl in an advanced English class, 'cause my secret admirer doesn't know the difference between *you're* and *your*. And then he had to spend five minutes explaining the difference between *you're* and *your* to Kevin.

Anyway, now we're down to just twenty-eight girls. On Monday, I'm going to go down the list and try talking to each of them, to see if I can figure out which one it is.

MAY 5

[mood: muggle-ish]

My parents just started reading the *Harry Potter* books to Sophie—last night, I heard them reading the beginning of the first book to her. Here's what I don't understand about Hogwarts: Okay, so the school has a sorting hat that can figure out each student's true nature, and assign him or her to the appropriate house, right? But there are four houses. Three of them—Gryffindor, Hufflepuff, and Ravenclaw—are full of normal people. And then there's Slytherin, which has NOTHING BUT EVIL PEOPLE. If I ran Hogwarts, when the sorting hat assigned a student to Slytherin, I'd send him home, or maybe to, like, wizard reform school. I mean, duh.

Ugh. So today I managed to talk to six of the girls on my list. I don't think any of them are the one. I asked Julie Kahn how she was doing and she said, "Who wants to know?" I asked Samantha Scanlon if I could borrow a pen, and she sighed and made

me give her a dollar as a deposit, so she could be sure to get it back. Three different girls, when they saw me coming, pretended their cell phone had just rung and they had to answer it, which was really obvious when Violet Paterson did it, because she doesn't even own a cell phone, so she used her calculator instead. And Nina Liu was really friendly to me, which I took as a good sign, until she

asked me, "Do you think your friend Kevin likes me?" Which is good news for Kevin, I guess, but doesn't help me.

OK. I give up. I tried talking to three more of the girls on my list. I asked Kate McLean, "How's it going?" and she told me, "None of your business." When I asked Sara Jacobsen what time it was, she said, "Time for you to stop bothering me." And Deb Chang just stared at me as I talked to her, then turned to one of her friends and said, "Did you hear something? It's like someone was speaking, but I didn't see anyone."

That's it. I'm done trying to figure out who it is. I'm going to spend my time doing other stuff. Like figuring out what you call a Hot Pocket when it gets cold. Is it a cold Hot Pocket? Or just a Cold Pocket?

Well, the secret admirer mystery's solved. I got another note in my locker today:

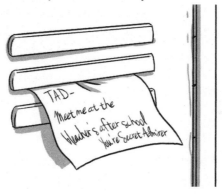

So I went down to the bleachers, and I waited, and I waited, and I waited, but nobody showed up—the only person there was Stu Lawrence, who also seemed to be just waiting around. So we started talking, and he asked me why I was hanging around, and so I told him about my secret admirer. And he got sort of pale and asked to see the note, so I showed it to him. And he said, "Is your locker near Tara-Ann Dillon's?" And I told him, yeah, I had the locker next to hers. And he said, "Aw, crap," and he turned super bright red.

And then neither of us said anything, but he just took the note out of my hand.

So I guess Stu Lawrence was accidentally my secret admirer. He asked me not to tell anyone about the whole thing. I told him that'd be fine by me.

In art today, Mrs. Sweeney gave us each a canvas and told us to paint "something that feels very familiar to you." Which seemed like kind of a dumb assignment, because why would anyone want a picture of something they see every day? "Boy, it's a good thing I painted that picture of my shoes! It saves me the trouble of looking down!" But Mrs. Sweeney's kind of weird and artsy like that. (She's a sculptor, and I remember one time, she showed us one of her sculptures and said it was called "Reclining Woman," but to all of us, it just looked like a pile of rusty metal. Chuck leaned over and said, "If she's in there, I hope that woman has a tetanus shot.")

Anyway, I decided to paint a picture of our fridge

at home, and I'd gotten pretty far along when Chuck looked over at it and said, "Why are you painting a robot?" Once he'd pointed it out, I realized he was right: It totally looked like a robot. In fact, it looked a lot more like a robot than a fridge.

So I tried starting over, and painted over it with white paint, but everything started smearing and running together and turning gray. I was worried I'd have to ask for another canvas, until I had a great idea: I'd paint over it with black paint, and put a yellow line down the middle of it, and then paint in a dead opossum. Which is totally familiar to me, because it's something I see from the school bus all the time. I'd painted it black and was just adding the yellow line for the divider when Mrs. Sweeney came by and said, "My, Tad! This looks interesting! What're you painting?" And I said, "The dividing line." And she said, "A dividing line? That feels familiar to you?" And I said, "Um, yeah." Then she got excited and said, "You feel divided? Torn? Ambivalent? Torn between two worlds?"

I could tell from the tone of her voice that there was only one right answer. So I said, "Yes. That is exactly what I feel." She got even more excited, and said, "This painting is the only one that truly fulfills the assignment!" Which is weird, because it just looks like this:

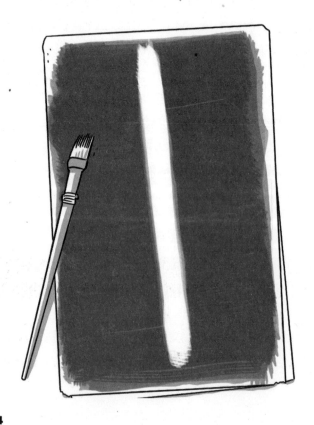

I still think it'd look a thousand times better with a dead opossum in the middle of it.

We went to the grocery store tonight, and I saw a little kid riding around in the shopping cart, in the backward-facing seat near the handle. I don't even remember the last time I sat in one of those. I mean, I know that there was a time when I was really little, and I used to sit in there and just chill out for the whole shopping trip. Then there was a time when I stopped, and I had to walk all the way around the store while my mom tried to figure out which of her coupons hadn't expired yet.

I kind of wish my mom had told me when I was taking my last ride in that shopping-cart seat. I think I would've enjoyed it more.

Tomorrow is Mother's Day, so Chuck and I went to the mall to find presents for our moms. I found a really good book for her, called *Drop 15 Pounds in 30 Days!*, because she's always talking about how much she wants to lose weight. But I showed it to my dad when I got home, and he took me back to the bookstore to exchange it. I asked him what I should exchange it for, and he said, "Anything else."

MAY 13　　　[mood: 　　happy]

Today was Mother's Day. Sophie and I got up early to make my mom breakfast in bed. We decided to make her French toast, and I think we did OK. I mean, the only bread we had left in the house was rye bread, so we had to use that. And we were out of milk, so we just mixed together some some non-dairy creamer and water. And we didn't have any vanilla, so Sophie crumbled up some Nilla Wafers and stirred them in. But my mom seemed to really like it—when we brought it up to her, she said that she wanted more maple syrup, and by the time we'd gone downstairs and gotten it and brought it back up, she'd eaten everything. I asked her if she wanted us to make some more, but she said no, she was full.

Big news: Chuck and I were walking home from school this afternoon when this dog started following us home. (Well, I guess it didn't start following us until Chuck gave it some of his leftover nachos.) Anyway, after we got to my house, the dog kept sitting outside and whining. At first, my mom said to leave it outside, and it'd get bored and find its way home. But it just sat there whining, and my mom said to let it in, because it was really distracting her from watching *So You Think You Can Dance* (which, by the way, is a stupid name for a show. It's like if, instead of *American Idol*, they'd called it *Nice Singing, Jerkface*).

Tomorrow, we're going to put up signs saying that we found the dog, to see if we can track down its owner. But if we can't, my mom said maybe we might keep it. I might have a dog! Here is a picture of it:

His name is Rex. It's short for Dogasaurus Rex.

Here is the first thing I have learned about having a dog in your house: Don't feed them nachos. Not ever.

Anyway. After spending the morning cleaning the living room rug, my dad and I went to the store and put up signs with a picture of Rex on it. I really hope nobody calls. (I tried leaving one digit off our phone number, but my dad noticed.)

You know what I bet would suck? If you died and went to heaven, but really hated harp music.

Well, it's been five days, and nobody's called to claim Rex. I think my parents are growing to like him, too. We've figured out that he knows how to fetch, sit, roll over, and stay. My mom says that means he probably has an owner, but I think it just means he's a really smart dog.

[mood: excited] **MAY 21**

This morning was a little exciting. We got a brand-new school bus for our ride to school. Rocky, our school bus driver, was super psyched about it. He said, "I've been asking the district for a new school bus for three years now." And then he whispered, "I wasn't supposed to say anything, but the brakes on our old bus were shot. It was just a rolling death trap."

I kind of wish he hadn't told me that.

Anyway, it's nice having a brand-new bus. It's the first time I've ever been in a school bus that didn't smell just a little bit like vomit mixed with orange-scented disinfectant. I wonder how long it'll last.

Rocky the bus driver

MAY 22 [mood: disappointed]

Well, this afternoon, I got an answer to my question. A school bus can go approximately thirty-one hours without smelling like vomit. Becky Keeton had a bad tuna-fish sandwich at lunch, and lost it just before my stop. When I was getting off the bus, Rocky was sadly getting out the paper towels

and the sawdust and the disinfectant. I looked at him and said, "It was nice while it lasted," and he sort of smiled and said, "Yeah, it was."

Hooray! Rex has been with us for eleven days now, and nobody's claimed him, so my parents said we're gonna keep him! Tomorrow, we're going to take him to the Lakeville Cat & Dog Hospital to get him checked out. Sophie got really excited about the idea that we were going to the Cat & Dog Hospital, until my mom explained that that just means "veterinary clinic," and not "a hospital where all the doctors are cats and dogs."

Great news about Rex: The vet said the dog seems healthy, he just needs to be fixed. (Sophie asked what *fixed* means. My mom said it means a dog needs to be repaired. I said, "Yeah, repaired by cutting off his—" but then my mom asked me whether I liked having my Wii, and whether I'd like to have it taken away for a month, and I stopped talking.)

MAY 28 [mood: happier]

Well, Rex is back from the vet. It's probably a good thing he doesn't know how stupid he looks with this cone on:

Sophie asked why he has to wear the cone. I told her it was so he could pick up satellite radio.

Ugh. Bad news. We got a call today. Turns out, Rex has an owner. Also, his name isn't Rex. It's Mr. Kensington. I guess his owners were off on a cruise for the past three weeks, and their dog-sitter didn't want to ruin their vacation, so she didn't call to tell them he was missing. The owners were super grateful—apparently, Rex is a purebred German Spitz, and he's, like, won prizes at dog shows. They said it was a good thing we found him, because they're planning on making a lot of money by breeding him. My parents just kind of looked at each other, and then my mom said, "Good luck with that."

[mood: roaaaaaar!] **MAY 30**

I don't get the plot of *Jurassic Park*. Like, if you're bringing back dinosaurs from the dead

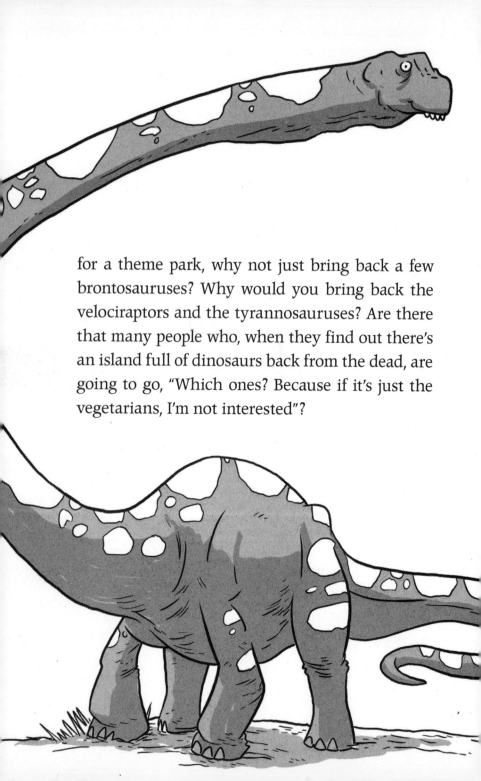

for a theme park, why not just bring back a few brontosauruses? Why would you bring back the velociraptors and the tyrannosauruses? Are there that many people who, when they find out there's an island full of dinosaurs back from the dead, are going to go, "Which ones? Because if it's just the vegetarians, I'm not interested"?

June

[mood:  excited]

Just one more week left of school before summer. I can't wait for vacation to start. Our teachers seem even more excited than we are—Mr. Parker was walking around the class whistling and humming today. And our principal, Dr. Evans, stopped Doug Spivak in the hallway to tell him that he'd managed to get a D-plus average, so he'd be going on to eighth grade. "Do you know what that means? We're almost done with you!" she said, and they both started jumping up and down happily. I guess it's nice that she cares so much about Doug.

JUNE 4 [mood: annoyed]

Oof. This morning, we found out that the seventh graders are all going to have to sing a song at the eighth graders' graduation on Friday afternoon. I guess it was an idea dreamed up by the chorus teacher, Mrs. Valeri, who's super mean—like, even the other teachers are afraid of her.

So we're all supposed to sing "I Believe I Can Fly." Which is just stupid—I thought the idea was, we were done with school for the year, so we didn't have to do what our teachers said anymore.

And if we have to sing a song, why does it have to be some lame song about some stupid guy who thinks he can fly? And worst of all, we have to rehearse it every day with Mrs. Valeri during our lunch period. I can't wait till I'm out of middle school and people can't force me to do stupid stuff I don't want to do ever again.

JUNE 5 [mood: even more annoyed]

We rehearsed our stupid song today at lunch. Mrs. Valeri kept getting angry at us because we weren't singing it right. She kept saying, "You're all off-key!" and I kept thinking: If we're all off-key, then isn't it possible that the key we're singing it in is the key that it should be in?

[mood: annoyed-er] **JUNE 6**

Today in rehearsal for the graduation song, Mrs. Valeri got really mad at Charlotte Regan for being "pitchy" and "sounding like a bag full of cats," until Charlotte started crying and left the room.

Mrs. Valeri said, "I'm sorry, but I just want to make sure the eighth graders have a good time at their graduation." I guess she doesn't care if anyone else has a good time at their graduation.

Rehearsal today was even worse than yesterday. Mrs. Valeri shouted at Chuck and me and said we were "ruining the song on purpose," and then said that anyone who she thought was "deliberately singing poorly" during graduation would get detention. I'm not even sure how you get detention during summer vacation, but Chuck and I agreed that we weren't going to take that risk. So tomorrow during the song, we're just going to mouth the lyrics.

Well, I'm now officially an eighth grader! We sang at graduation tonight, and we're done.

But that wasn't even the best part. The best part was, at lunch, Chuck told some other people at our table about our plan to mouth the words. And I guess they told some other people, and they told some other people, and everyone agreed that it was a really good idea. Because tonight, at the graduation ceremony, when it came time for all of us to sing, every single kid in our class just mouthed the words to the song. All you could hear was Mrs. Valeri playing the piano, and this slight smacking sound of everyone's mouths opening and closing.

My dad said it was the funniest thing he'd ever seen. Mrs. Valeri ran after everyone afterward, threatening to keep them in summer school, until our principal, Dr. Evans, put her hand on Mrs. Valeri's shoulder and said, "Give it a rest, Constance."

It was a good day.

JUNE 9 [mood: free!]

Yesterday was the last day of school! Yeeeeeeeeeeeeeeeeeeeeeeeeeeee-ha! Summer!!!!! This is going to be the best summer ever!

I spent the day doing nothing but watching TV and playing video games. I could get used to three months of this.

Another day just sitting on the couch doing nothing. Watched *The Shawshank Redemption* on TNT twice in a row. I think *The Shawshank Redemption* may be the only movie they own.

[mood: depressed]   **JUNE 11**

Today, my dad came home while I was watching *The Shawshank Redemption* for the fourth time and said, "How'd you enjoy your weekend off?" And I was like, "Huh?" And he said, "Well, you know that you're getting a summer job, right? We're not going to just let you sit here and rot your brain for three months. Besides, working teaches you valuable lessons." I told him that I'd been working really hard for nine months straight, and didn't I deserve three months off to recover? He just laughed and laughed and laughed, and when Mom came home, he made me repeat it to her, and then they both laughed together for a really long time.

JUNE 13 [mood: frustrated]

Well, I went to the local newspaper today to see if they needed anyone to deliver papers for them. The woman there gave me an application to fill  out, and so I did. And then she asked me whether I had a bike, and where I went to school, and what my favorite subjects were, and what hours I was available to work. And then she told me that they weren't hiring anybody, because they had all the paperboys they needed. I asked her why she'd gone to the trouble of asking me all those questions. She just shrugged and said, "Nobody ever comes to visit me in the circulation department."

JUNE 16 [mood: nervous]

Father's Day is tomorrow. I never know what to get my dad. Today while he was watching a baseball game, I went in to ask him what he wanted, and he said, "Just a little peace and quiet."

Which seemed like an odd thing to ask for as a present, but I went to the store and bought him five sets of earplugs.

JUNE 17 [mood: frustrated]

Father's Day is today. My dad really seemed to like the gift I'd gotten him—he said to my mom, "I can use these when we visit your family!" She didn't seem to think that was funny at all.

Today, I noticed something weird on a dollar bill: Next to George Washington's picture, there's a tiny signature. But it's not George Washington's signature—it's the Secretary of the Treasury's, whoever that is.

As best I can tell, his name is Hnnnny Nnn Pnnlnjn.

Being Secretary of the Treasury seems like a pretty cool job—you get to sign all the money. I wonder if part of the job requirement is that you have a good, official-looking signature. Like, I bet Traci Williams from my class could never be Secretary of the Treasury, because she dots the *i*'s in her name with hearts. Nobody would trust money with this on it:

I went to the food court at the mall today, where the Cinnabon manager told me I was too young for them to hire. Stupid Cinnabon. I'm glad they didn't hire me. If the manager's any indication, everyone who works there winds up fat, covered with zits, and reeking of cinnamon.

Great news! I got a job at the Hot Dog Pound! They're that hot-dog place up by the interstate, and I went in today because they had a "Help Wanted" sign, and they had an opening! I asked if I was too young, and the guy behind the counter said, "You're sixteen, right?" And I said, "No, I'm thirteen." And he said, "What's that? You said you're sixteen?" in a way that sort of suggested that that was the right answer. So I told him yes. The only weird part is, he asked me how tall I was. When I told him, "I'm five-four and a half," he said, "Perfect. Try not to grow before tomorrow." Who knew hot-dog restaurants had height requirements?

[mood: exhausted] JUNE 24

So I went to work today. I wore a pair of khakis and a button-down shirt, because Mom said it would impress the boss. But I shouldn't have bothered dressing up, because I spent the day wearing a hot-dog costume.

Let me say that again: I spent the day *wearing a hot-dog costume.*

It turns out that was the job—to stand out in front of the restaurant as their mascot and wave at cars as they drive by. I can understand why the last guy to have this job quit: The costume is cramped and hot and hard to see out of, and it smells like someone else's feet. Plus, in case I didn't mention this: It's a giant hot dog.

This is way worse than Cinnabon could ever be.

[mood: exhausted]   **JUNE 25**

Today, during my fifteen-minute lunch break, Pam from the drive-thru told me what really happened to the guy who was in the suit before me: He didn't quit—he passed out from heatstroke. She said he just kind of weaved all over the parking lot and then fell down with his legs in the air. "It was really funny," she

said, and then realized who she was talking to and was all, "Oh, but I'm sure it wouldn't be funny if it happened to you."

I'm trying to drink lots of fluids so I don't get heatstroke, but the restaurant makes us pay for the drinks we buy—even water! And since I'm only making 7 bucks an hour—5 bucks after taxes—and a drink is $1.75, I think I could wind up losing money this summer. Dad's right: A summer job *does* teach valuable lessons. Like, for instance: Work sucks.

JUNE 26 [mood: humiliated]

My manager, Sean, came out today and told me to wave and dance more. "Nobody wants to eat at a place where the food looks depressed," he said. "Look happy!" I pointed out that if I were really a hot dog, I wouldn't be happy to stand and wave in front of a restaurant where my fellow frankfurters were being eaten. And he said, "Maybe you're a really dumb hot dog, and you haven't figured it out yet." Great. I'm going to spend the summer not just being a hot dog, but being a really stupid hot dog.

Sophie left for camp today. This is her first time going to sleepaway camp, and she was afraid of being homesick. I told her that homesickness was nothing to worry about, and that what she should really be afraid of are the Forest Strangler and the Summer Camp Claw-Handed Serial Killer and the Feral Wombats Who Are Able to Open Doors. I think her first night at sleepaway camp's gonna be great.

So I haven't told any of my friends what I'm doing for a summer job, and today, Chuck and Kevin came to the Hot Dog Pound for lunch. I could see them through the peephole in my costume, but they couldn't see me. And I could hear them pretending to sneeze and saying "Wiener! Wiener!" behind my back. I don't know which is worse: that they did that to me, or that, if I weren't inside the stupid costume, I'd probably be with them doing the exact same thing.

I got a reprimand at work today. I don't think I was doing anything too wrong, but Sean said that I couldn't whisper to customers as they entered the restaurant, "You're eating my babies." I considered suggesting that, instead, I could yell "Bite me!" at people, but he seemed pretty annoyed with me already.

Well, this was my last day at the Hot Dog Pound. Apparently, I passed out in the parking lot and Pam dragged me inside. It turns out I was horribly dehydrated. Sean promised to give me two weeks' pay if I didn't sue, and my dad said, "Don't worry, we won't make you find another job." Which made me really happy, until he said, "There's a lot of chores that need doing around the house, anyway." So . . . I'll still be working, just not getting paid. Great.

July

Spent today drinking Gatorade and recovering from yesterday's dehydration incident. Watched a double feature of *Night at the Museum* and *Night at the Museum 2* on TV, then fell asleep and had a weird dream about a movie called *Night at the Zoo*, where Ben Stiller's a security guard at a zoo where, at night, all the animals magically turn into stuffed dioramas. It was kind of a boring dream, actually.

JULY 4

Today's the Fourth of July. My dad asked me how I was feeling, and I said, "Pretty good," and he said, "Great! You can go clean the gutters!" I told him that, in the spirit of Independence Day, I shouldn't have to do anything I didn't want to. He said that that would only be true if he were forcing me to pay taxes without representation, or quartering soldiers in my room.

[mood: happy]

JULY 6

Hooray! I was out mowing our lawn today, and some woman was driving by and asked me how much I charge per lawn. I guess she thought I was some sort of lawn-mowing service. I tried to think fast, and told her $15. She said, "Wow! $15? That's so cheap!" And then she hired me to mow her lawn.

So the good news is, someone's going to pay me for the chores my parents have been making me do for free.

Although the bad news is, I really, really wish I'd said $25.

I mowed that lady's lawn today, and she seemed pretty happy with it. She said she had some other friends who need yard work done, and she asked if she could give them my number. I told her yes. Then I started thinking that I could turn this into an actual business, so I took the money she paid me, went to Kinko's, and made some signs to advertise my service. It took a few tries:

Lawnmowing is really a much longer word than you would think it is.

My arms are sore. I spent the whole afternoon mowing the lawn and trimming hedges for our neighbor Mrs. Graham. I think hedges are stupid— I told Mrs. Graham that when I have a house, I'll have a yard full of cactuses. And she said, "Cacti. The plural is cacti." And I told her that if that were the case, then wouldn't more than one waitress be a group of waitri? She muttered, "Smart-ass," and paid me.

Here's what I've learned after three days of doing yard work:

- Mosquito repellent doesn't work.
- If you're applying sunscreen, it's really important to do it evenly. Otherwise, you'll wind up with a big red splotch on your face, and your mom and dad will spend a whole dinner trying to figure out what country it's shaped like, no matter how many times you ask them to stop.

- Mowing lawns makes your back super sore.
- Some people have much bigger lawns than others, so it's really, really stupid to charge a flat rate.
- Tylenol, sunscreen, mosquito repellent, and gasoline all cost a lot of money, which eats into your profits.

JULY 11 [mood:  cranky]

I just got back from putting up some more of my flyers at the supermarket. On the way home, I saw a new person out in front of the Hot Dog Pound in the hot-dog suit. I wonder how many employees they go through in a summer.

[mood:  sore] **JULY 12**

Argh. I was supposed to go to Six Flags with Chuck today, but this morning I woke up too sore to even move. So instead, I stayed home and sat on the couch all day, taking Tylenol and watching TV. At one point, I dropped the remote behind the couch and it hurt too much to get up and reach for it, so I wound up having to sit there, watching all of *The Lake House* and half of *The Sisterhood of the Traveling Pants*, before my parents came home.

I kind of miss just going to school.

I went down to the supermarket today to put up more of my flyers, and just as I got there, I saw a guy pulling down the ones I put up two days ago. I told him to stop, and he seemed sort of embarrassed, and said he was sorry, but he runs a lawn-mowing service, and I was really cutting into his business. I guess I charge only, like, one-quarter of what he does, so a lot of his

Frank's
Lawn Care *now only three and a half times the price of that one kid!*

customers went over to me.

I felt kind of bad for him, and then I thought of an idea: I don't like mowing lawns, and he doesn't like losing customers. So I told him that I'd give up my lawnmowing business if he'd agree to pay me $7.50 for every lawn I didn't mow. He said that sounded fair to him. So now I work for Frank's Lawn Care as a lawn nonmower.

I may have the best summer job ever.

JULY 14 [mood: frantic]

So tonight was kind of crazy. I was sitting around watching TV when my dad came home to find that Sophie had mailed a big envelope home from camp. He opened it up, and it was a construction-paper card that said "Happy Birthday, Mom!!!" That's when both my dad and I realized that we'd forgotten my mom's birthday, so he grabbed his car keys and we went to the mall—he found her some perfume and a Michael Bublé CD, and I found a kiosk called "The Perfect Gift! Your Astrological Sign on a Mug!" I told the guy there that my mom's birthday was today, and he gave me a box. It wasn't until my mom opened it up that I realized that not all astrological signs look good on mugs.

Why would you even sell that?

Sophie's been at camp for two weeks now, and I have to say, I'm beginning to miss having her around. Not so much because I miss having her annoy me, but because she always ate all the strawberry in the Neapolitan ice cream. With her gone, my mom's saying, "I refuse to throw away perfectly good ice cream," so my dad and I have to eat our way through the strawberry before my mom will buy a new carton of it.

I was over at Chuck's house tonight. His older brother, Sid, is home for the summer from college—

he's a professional amateur skateboarder, but in the meantime, he's working as a busboy at Applebee's. He showed us the tattoo that he got of the Tony Hawk company logo on his bicep. It looks really cool, and we all agreed it sucks that his manager at Applebee's makes him wear long-sleeved shirts to cover it up whenever he's working.

So sullen!

Coolest guy EVER?! I say yes!

When I got home, I asked my mom when I could get a tattoo, and she said, "When I've been dead at least five years."

That seems like a really long time to wait.

Sophie got back from camp today. We went to pick her up at the elementary-school parking lot, where the bus dropped her off. She ran over and hugged my mom and dad and said, "I missed you guys soooooo much!" Then she turned to me and whispered, "Hi, Tad. Do you have the $375 you owe me?"

I'd kind of forgotten that today was the due date to repay my loan from Sophie. I went to my room and collected all my earnings from this summer so far: I had just enough to pay back Sophie, with $8.27 left over. Sophie took it and said, "A pleasure doing business with you."

I really hope that when Sophie grows up, she uses her powers for good and not for evil.

I went to the dentist today for a checkup. I don't think my dentist likes me very much. It's partly my fault. I called him "Mr. Park." And he said, "It's

Dr. Park. I'm a doctor." And I said, "Really? Dentists are doctors?" And he said, "Yes, we are." And I said, "But you just deal with teeth." And he said, "Teeth are part of your body. We're doctors," and seemed kind of mad. Afterward, he told me I had two cavities, and added, "So I guess you'll be back at this doctor's office soon, for a doctor's appointment, with me, your doctor."

I'm realizing that it might not have been a good idea to annoy the guy who's going to be drilling into my teeth.

It's raining out, so there's nothing to do. Sophie and I spent a little while playing Hangman. Hangman's sort of a strange game, if you think about it. Supposedly, the idea is to avoid having your little stick-figure guy get hanged, right? But pretty much as soon as you've gotten even one letter wrong, you're not just dead—you're decapitated.

I feel like once your head's been hung, it really doesn't matter if they hang the rest of you.

[mood: tired] **JULY 20**

Another rainy day. Watched *The Wizard of Oz* with Sophie. There's all sorts of stuff I don't understand about that movie. Like for instance:

When Dorothy lands in Oz, three members of the Lollipop Guild show up right away to welcome her, and they're like, "We represent the Lollipop Guild, and on behalf of the Lollipop Guild, we welcome you to Munchkinland." How did the Lollipop Guild decide so quickly who would represent them? Like, somehow, within seconds of a house landing in their town, did they have a meeting to vote on who should go welcome the person in the house? Or does the Lollipop Guild have a standing committee on People-in-Flying-House-Welcoming?

Also, why doesn't the Wicked Witch of the West put diapers on her flying monkeys? As Mrs. Shelton learned the hard way during our fifth-grade field trip to the zoo, monkeys like to fling their poop at people. And flying monkeys would probably just poop all over everything. Sure, the Wicked Witch's monkeys seem pretty well trained. But if I had a flying-monkey army, I'd make sure to keep them all diapered, just in case.

And also: If having water thrown on you were going to make you melt, wouldn't you be a little more careful about leaving buckets of water lying around?

Aside from that, though, it's a pretty good movie.

JULY 21

[mood:  curious]

I wonder: Is there any law against changing your first name to "Doctor"? Because it seems like there should be.

[mood: still curious] **JULY 23**

I wonder when chickens figure out that they can't fly. Like, does every chicken go through a period of looking at ducks and going, "One day, that'll be me," before eventually realizing that, nope, it's never going to happen for them?

JULY 24

[mood: sympathetic]

I bet chickens get angry at birds who *can* fly but who choose to walk.

If breakfast cereal is so popular, how come nobody makes dinner cereal? I'd eat it.

[mood: happy] **JULY 28**

Today, Chuck and I invented a fun new game called Guitar Villain. You play Guitar Hero, but instead of trying to get the highest possible score, you see if you can get the lowest possible score. If you play it just right, a song will sound like "SQUONK SQUONK SQUONK SQUONK SQUONK" for three straight minutes. We played it for about half an

hour before my mom came downstairs and told us that if we didn't stop making that awful noise, she'd make us go outside to get some fresh air.

JULY 30 [mood: pensive]

Dog the Bounty Hunter is an interesting show, but it'd be ten times more interesting if it were about a bounty-hunting dog.

August

Today on TV, I saw a guy say that a goldfish has a memory span of seven seconds. It made me feel kind of sorry for them, because I bet the only thing that ever goes through their mind is, "Oh my God, I'm drowning! No, wait, I have gills. Oh my God, I'm drowning! No, wait, I have gills. Oh my God, I'm drowning! No, wait, I have gills."

Sophie has her best friend, Amy, over for a sleepover tonight—they're both sleeping in a tent in the living room. Originally, they were planning on going camping in our backyard, but then Amy said she was too scared to do it, because she might get bitten by a rattlesnake. My dad tried to talk her out of it by pointing out that rattlesnakes don't even live in our area, and besides, "You're twenty times likelier to be hit by lightning than bit by a rattlesnake." And the good news is, Amy's not afraid of rattlesnakes anymore. The bad news is, she's now completely terrified of getting hit by lightning. Seriously. She may never leave our house.

[mood: spacey] AUGUST 4

I've been watching a lot of *Battlestar Galactica* reruns lately. If you've never seen it, *Battlestar Galactica* is about people from a planet millions of miles away from Earth, and they have pretty much the same clothes, language, appliances, and expressions as we do. The only differences are that they use a made-up swear word that you can say on television, and the shape of the paper they use is different.

How to Tell If You Are on the Other Side of the Universe with Starbuck and Apollo!

On the other side of the universe paper!

Our paper!

I wonder what that show's fan conventions are like. Does everyone just show up carrying around a piece of paper with the corners cut off, so that people know they're dressed up as characters from the show?

I went to the mall with my mom today to finally buy my summer reading books, *Animal Farm* and *The Great Gatsby*. My mom also dragged me along to Bed Bath & Beyond, which is such a stupid name for a store. The "Beyond" part makes it sound like they sell, like, tickets to Narnia or something, but it turns out, "Beyond" just means "forks and scented candles."

I rented season one of *24* yesterday to see if I could watch it all in a day. It doesn't take a full 24 hours—it turns out that each hour is only around forty minutes, because the episodes on the DVDs don't have commercials. Which is sort of weird, since the show's supposed to take place in real time. I wonder what the characters do for those extra twenty minutes of every hour. Maybe that's when Jack Bauer gets to pee.

I had to hide what I was doing from my mom and dad, 'cause I knew they wouldn't approve. So I spent most of the day in my room watching the DVDs on my computer. But I took a quick break for dinner, and asked my sister for the salt by saying, "Quick—the salt—send it over here! There's no time to lose! Pass the salt! PASS THE SALT NOW!" That's when my parents searched my room to see if I was on drugs, found the *24* episodes, and confiscated them.

AUGUST 7 [mood: bored]

Thirty pages into *The Great Gatsby*, and I'm still waiting for him to do something great. He just seems like a boring rich guy to me.

 [mood: sleepy] ## AUGUST 8

Bad news: Sophie found my copy of *Animal Farm*, thought the cover was cute, and read it. (She's Gifted and Talented, and reads at a ninth-grade

level. I know this because she keeps telling everyone she meets.) Now she keeps waking everyone
up with nightmares about how the evil pigs killed
Boxer the horse.

There is one bright side, though. I got her to
tell me everything that happened in the book,
and now I don't have to read it. I tried to get her
interested in *The Great Gatsby* by telling her it was
about animals, too, but she didn't believe me when
I told her everyone in it was a weasel.

No weasels (exploding or otherwise...)

Well thank you for small mercies!

My family's leaving on vacation today. We're going to spend a week in Florida, visiting my Grandma Judy in her new retirement home. Well, actually, just five days with Grandma Judy—it's a twelve-hour, two-day drive each way. My dad's excited about it, because Grandma Judy's his mom. And Sophie's excited about it, because my grandma takes her shopping and they sit together at night and watch home-makeover shows and eat ice cream together. My mom and I are less excited about it. I hate going shopping, and I hate home-makeover shows, and my grandma always calls me "Taddy," which I used to be called back when I was, like, five, but nobody calls me anymore. And my mom doesn't like my grandma. She never says so, but I can tell that she doesn't, through little hints she drops, like asking my dad, "Why do we have to go visit her?" and always sighing heavily halfway through my Grandma Judy's name, so it comes out as "Grandma . . . (sigh) . . . Judy." I'm good at picking up on small clues like that.

OK. My mom just came into my room and asked,

"Are you packed yet for the trip to Grandma . . . (sigh) . . . Judy's?" So I guess I should go pack. I'm packing my swim trunks—the one nice thing about going to Grandma Judy's is at least I'll get to go to the beach. It'll be fun to go swimming. Plus, I'm super pale, so it'll be a chance to maybe get a tan just in time for school.

AUGUST 10 [mood: exhausted]

Uuuuuuugh. Today was a looooooooong day of driving. The first few hours of the trip were OK, because Sophie was watching a DVD of *The Little Mermaid* and I was playing on my GamePort XL. But a few hours in, the batteries died on my sister's DVD player. My sister started whining, and my mom said to my dad, "I thought I told you to recharge them!" But my dad was like, "No, that was your job! My job was to drive to my mother's!" My mom was like, "Well, it was your idea to go visit her!" and my sister just kept whining because the movie had stopped before the ending. I said, "You've seen the movie, like, fifty times. Did you forget how it ends? She gets legs." And my mom snapped, "Tad! Be nice to your sister!" which I thought was really strange, because I was the only one in the car not whining or shouting at anyone.

So then my mom told me to let Sophie play with my GamePort, but Sophie didn't want to play with it, because it didn't have any games involving princesses or cake, which are the only kinds of games that Sophie likes to play. And so my dad announced that we'd be entertaining ourselves the way that he did on car trips when he was a kid, by competing to see who could count more cows on their side of the car. Which is a stupid game, because winning and losing really depends on how many cows there happen to be on the side of the road. Sophie was cheating, which made me really angry, until I remembered that I didn't actually care who won the game.

Anyway. We just stopped at a motel for the night. It's the second motel we stopped at. We checked into the first one, and Sophie got all excited because there were machines on the beds that made them vibrate if you put in a quarter, and my mom just picked up our bags, went to the car, and told my dad, "Find another motel." I don't know why. I think vibrating beds sound like fun.

Well, this morning, we drove the rest of the way to Grandma Judy's place. She seemed really happy to see us. Or happy to see my dad and my sister, anyway. She gave my dad a big hug, and turned to Sophie and said, "Sophie! You've grown so much! You're such the little lady! I've got a whole *Trading*

Spaces marathon saved up for us to watch, and a carton of Neapolitan with your name on it!" Then she turned to me and said, "Taddy, it's nice to see you," and to my mom she said, "Well, you've certainly put on some weight!" My mom was still trying to think of a response when Grandma Judy started carrying Sophie's suitcase up to her room.

After all that, by the time we got all settled in, it was too late to go to the beach. But my mom said we can go tomorrow.

AUGUST 12 [mood: bored to death]

Man, this trip sucks. It rained today, so we wound up skipping the beach. But Grandma Judy turned to Sophie and said, "You know what the rain is good for?" And Sophie said, "Outlet shopping!" So we went shopping at the outlet mall. Outlet malls are like regular malls, only bigger, and without the only stuff that makes malls bearable, like food courts or bookstores where you can look through comic books.

I was getting really hungry, so I was happy when Grandma Judy said that we would stop at the Cheesecake Factory on the way home. But it wasn't the Cheesecake Factory restaurant, it was an outlet store for a factory that makes cheese-cakes. Grandma Judy bought two, but wouldn't let me eat any, because she was going to freeze them "for when company came." Anyway, the weather guy on TV said that it'd be sunny tomorrow, and my mom promised that, no matter what, we'd go to the beach.

Argh. Today we were supposed to go to the beach, but instead, Grandma Judy said she had a surprise for us: She wanted us to meet her friend William. He's also super old, and he lives down the hall from her in the retirement home. He seemed OK, even though he did try playing "I've got your nose!" with Sophie and me, and pulling quarters out of our ears, which even Sophie's too old for. I kept thinking that it would be funny to grab his dentures and go, "I've got your teeth!" but I knew everyone would be mad.

Also, I didn't want to

touch his dentures.

Anyway, hanging out with William was fine. The only weird thing was that my dad kept saying over and over, "You never mentioned that you'd made a friend," which I thought was strange, because why would Grandma Judy call my dad every time she makes a friend?

AUGUST 14   [mood: happy]

Well, we finally went to the beach today. We just got back, and it was a lot of fun—I went swimming, and helped Sophie build a sand castle, and we picked up, like, fifty shells. The only downside is, I didn't get a tan at all—which is weird, because I wasn't even wearing any sunscreen. (I knew I didn't have much time to get tan, so I figured I'd wait till I was a little brown, and then put the sunscreen on.) I just stayed super white all day long. Anyway, I'm going to go ask Grandma Judy to turn up the air-conditioning, because for some reason, it suddenly feels really hot in here.

Owwwwwwwwwwwwwwwwwwwwwwwwwwww.

I am covered in a giant, awful sunburn. Turns out, it takes a few hours for the sun to really change your skin's color, so last night, my whole body turned from white, to pink, to red, to redder. Sophie spent a while last night trying to decide what color I was, and finally chose "Kool-Aid Man."

We were going to go back to the beach today, but it hurts whenever the sun touches my skin, so instead, I'm spending the day indoors, covered in Noxzema, sitting in the living room in a lawn chair because Grandma Judy doesn't want the Noxzema getting on her furniture's plastic coverings. I've been stuck here all day, watching TLC home-renovation shows with Sophie and Grandma Judy—I keep dozing off, and then waking up to them squealing any time someone sponge-paints a wall or adds a sconce.

This is officially the worst vacation ever.

AUGUST 16 [mood:  miserable]

Spent the day driving back from Grandma Judy's place. We're halfway home now. Nothing to report, except that there are 78 cows on the left side of the car on the way home and—according to Sophie—394 cows on the right side.

Oh, and my sunburn is now peeling super badly. It's itchy, but I'm trying not to touch it, in order to see if I can just slip out of a Tad-shaped skin husk, like a snake.

[mood: relieved] AUGUST 17

Sooo nice to be home again. Crawled into bed and slept for twelve hours. Never want to see a home-decorating show, ice cream, or the sun ever again.

AUGUST 18 [mood: annoyed]

Ugh. Our neighbor Dawn is here, hanging out with my mom, so I'm hiding up in my room. I don't like

Dawn. For one thing, she smokes, which is just gross. My mom will usually hang out with her on the back porch, so that our whole house doesn't wind up smelling all Dawn-y. But the main reason I don't like her is that she begins, like, half her sentences by saying "Frankly" or "To be perfectly honest" or "Truthfully," which just weirds me out, because it always gives you the sense that, whenever she *doesn't* begin a sentence that way, then she's just totally lying.

AUGUST 19   [mood: curious]

Sophie's been reading a book all about unicorns, but it doesn't answer my big question about them: Why'd we stop at one horn? If you're going to make up a mythical animal, why not make up bicorns, tricorns, quadricorns, and so on? I think that the octocorn would actually be kind of a cool animal.

Today was Sophie's birthday. She's having a party this weekend, but for her actual birthday, we went out to dinner to her favorite restaurant: Red Lobster. I don't get the restaurant name Red Lobster. Aren't all lobsters red? It's not like they have a rival called Green Lobster.

Actually, on second thought, I bet the way Red Lobster happened was, the founder originally was going to call his restaurant Lobster. And so he painted it on the sign, and realized that the word *Lobster* looked kind of stupid up there all alone–like, it didn't look like it was a sign for a restaurant that served lob-ster, it just looked like a sign a lobster would put on his house. But there wasn't a lot of room to add anything, so he just squeezed the word *Red* above it.

My mom's running around getting ready for Sophie's eighth birthday. She's having a Barbie-themed party. That was her third choice. Her first choice was to have a princess-themed party, but then my mom told her that if that was the theme of the party, it couldn't just be HER being a princess—she had to let the other girls be princesses, too. Her second choice was a Lady GaGa–themed party, and both my mom and dad told her absolutely not. So it's a Barbie-themed party. I'm going to try to be out of the house as long as I can.

[mood: curious] **AUGUST 25**

I bet the hardest part about being Bruce Banner isn't the moment when you turn into the Hulk. It's when you're done being angry, and you calm down, and suddenly you're naked in the middle of a whole lot of rubble, and someone's looking at you like, "Um, that's my car you just threw." I bet that part never gets any easier.

Well, today was Sophie's party. I went to the mall and managed to miss almost the whole thing—only one of Sophie's friends was still there when I got home, Brenda Winters, who was waiting for her mom to pick her up. She'd had too much cake and ice cream and kept saying, over and over, "I think I'm gonna throw up!" My mom looked really nervous, because Brenda was sitting on the couch that's not Scotchgarded.

Anyway, for her birthday, my parents got Sophie a hamster, which is totally unfair, because they never let me have a pet. This is what her hamster looks like: ———————————▷

Mr. Squeakers

His name is Thunderclaw. Sophie calls him Mr. Squeakers, but he and I both know his name is Thunderclaw.

Thunderclaw!

Chuck came over today, and we sneaked into Sophie's room to play with Thunderclaw when she was out at her oboe lesson. I think he's a really smart hamster, because Chuck made a little maze out of Legos, and Thunderclaw figured out how to get through it in no time. Chuck's coming over tomorrow, when Sophie and my parents are at her oboe recital, and we're going to build a hamster-size obstacle course to test Thunderclaw's strength and agility.

Oh, man. Today was a long day. Chuck and I were putting Thunderclaw through the obstacle course, and he'd already finished the swimming portion in the bathroom sink, and the ice-skating portion inside a carton of sherbet we found in the back of the freezer. But then, during the Road Rally, when we had him in my radio-controlled car, Chuck took a turn too hard and it slammed into the coffee table. Thunderclaw went flying off somewhere in the direction of the sofa, and we couldn't find him, despite spending a long time diagramming where he could have landed:

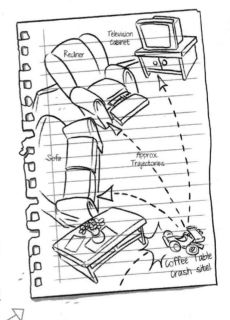

Finally, we gave up on finding him, and ran down to Pets-a-Million to find a replacement for

Thunderclaw before Sophie got home. I think the one we found looks a lot like him, especially after we added some spots with a brown magic marker:

Gotta go—I hear Sophie and my folks getting home.

Mr. Squeakers II

Good news! Sophie thinks Thunderclaw II is her original hamster! Although she did tell Mom and Dad that Mr. Squeakers is suddenly "a whole lot bitey-er."

Um. Well. Today brought good news and bad news. The good news is, we found Thunderclaw I. The bad news is, he was in my mom's Rice Krispies.

I guess, after we lost him, he ran into the kitchen

and climbed into a cereal box for some food, and then he couldn't climb out again. So this morning Mom was pouring herself some cereal, and suddenly she screamed, because there in the bowl, with his four tiny paws in the air, was the lifeless body of Thunderclaw I. Sophie started crying and

ran to her room, and then a minute later, she came back down to tell us that it couldn't be Thunderclaw, because he was still in his cage. And mom said, "Well, how did a hamster that looks just like him wind up in my cereal?" I tried to suggest that maybe it was a prize—like, they were giving away one free dead hamster in every box of Rice Krispies.

Mom stared at me for a really long time, and then she asked, "Is there something you want to tell us?"

And I answered honestly: No. There was absolutely nothing I wanted to tell her.

September

School starts on Tuesday, so today I had to go back-to-school shopping with my mom. (She won't let me go on my own. Apparently, you buy one "I'm with Stupid" T-shirt and suddenly you're not allowed to buy clothes by yourself anymore.)

We spent the whole day going from store to store, and she made me try stuff on, then come out of the changing room to show her. The worst moment came at Marshalls, when I tried on some jeans and she announced, "Those look like they're too tight in the crotch!" That's when I looked up and saw that April Dawson was shopping nearby, and she was trying hard not to crack up. And then I realized April was with her mom, and her mom was *also* trying not to crack up.

It's too late for me to change schools this year. I checked. But I told my mom that I'm not going shopping with her ever again.

Well, today I found out what's worse than going shopping with my mom: not going shopping with her. She brought home a bunch of clothes from TJ Maxx and said, "I bought you some school clothes!

I'll return whatever doesn't fit!" Some of the stuff was OK, but some of it was really ugly. She bought me a purple sweater-vest, and I told her I didn't like it and wanted her to return it, but she insisted that I keep it, because, she said, "It makes you look so handsome."

I don't even understand sweater-vests. Like, are they sweaters for people whose arms don't get cold?

I've hidden it in the back of my closet. Hopefully, she'll forget she bought it.

SEPTEMBER 3 [mood: sad]

Today's Labor Day, so my parents have the day off work. I'm not sure why. It's Labor Day, so shouldn't they have to work extra-hard instead?

Unless maybe it's called Labor Day in salute to anyone who's ever gone through labor.

No, wait. That's what Mother's Day is for.

(I'm spending my time thinking about stuff like this to try and distract myself from the fact that summer is over, and it's my first day of eighth grade tomorrow. It's not working.)

Today was my first day of eighth grade. It's cool to finally be the oldest kids in school—we get to use the eighth-grade lockers, which are over by the lunchroom. But for fun, Chuck and I walked by the hallway where the sixth graders have their lockers, just to watch them wandering around looking lost, or running to get Mr. Fox, the custodian, to open their lockers because they forgot the combination. Speaking of which: Chuck taught me a neat trick to remember your locker combination. You can hide it in your math notebook by putting it into a fake equation. Like, if your combination is 9-30-6, just write in your notebook "9 + 30 = 6." That way, if anyone finds your notebook, they won't

Sigh. Every year . . .

figure out that's your locker combination—they'll just think that you're sort of dumb and not very good at math.

SEPTEMBER 5 [mood: frustrated]

Arrrgh. Today I figured out the problem with Chuck's math-notebook method for holding on to your locker combination: It doesn't work if your math notebook is inside your locker.

[mood: excited] **SEPTEMBER 6**

The big news at school is that there's a new girl in our class. In homeroom, Mrs. DeWitt said, "I want you all to give a big Lakeville Pirates welcome to Jenny Bachman. Her family just moved here from Idaho, so she's starting school a little late. Welcome, Jenny!"

After homeroom, I said to Jenny, "So what's Idaho like?" And she said, "Actually, I'm from Ohio. Mrs. DeWitt got it wrong, but I didn't want to correct her." And I said, "Oh," and then there was an awkward pause, and I was about to say, "What's Ohio like?" but then Mark O'Keefe came over and said hi, and she said, "Hi! I like your Iron Man shirt. He's my favorite superhero. Well, Marvel super-hero, anyway." And they walked off together talking about comic books.

So: She's cute, she's nice, she likes comic books. And I wasted my chance to talk to her, all because Mrs. DeWitt confuses Idaho with Ohio. Stupid geography.

Jenny Bachman (!!!)
Not from Idaho!

Cute!

Loves comics!

SEPTEMBER 7 [mood:  smitten]

Chuck and I spent a long time at lunch today arguing about which of the X-Men has a lamer superpower, Storm or Iceman. Afterward, Jenny Bachman came up to us and said, "I'm sorry—I couldn't help overhearing. Clearly, it's Iceman. Storm can at least control the weather. What can Iceman do? Make your drink cold? Still, nobody's as lame as Gambit. What kind of superhero has playing cards as a weapon? If you wanted to kill him, all you'd have to do is attack him with fifty-three guys."

Then she walked away. Chuck and I are both totally in love.

SEPTEMBER 10 [mood:  dread]

This morning, I was heading out the door to school, and my mom said, "You know what would look nice with that shirt? That sweater-vest I got you. Why don't you go put it on?"

I told her I was late for school, so I couldn't change. But now I know: My mom hasn't forgotten the sweater-vest. She's going to make me wear it. It's only a matter of time.

Tonight, at dinner, my mom said, "You know what I hear is really 'in' this season? Sweater-vests. All the big celebrities are wearing them now." And I said, "But I don't want to wear a sweater-vest," and she said, "Trust me on this, you'll look really cute in it. The girls will like it!"

After dinner, my dad took me aside and said, "Don't even try fighting her on this." He's got a point: My mom thinks she knows a lot about fashion, so she can get really obsessed with how we dress. She once wrestled Sophie for ten minutes to get her into a yellow polka-dotted dress for Easter. (Although, to be fair, Sophie did look nice in it.)

[mood: annoyed] SEPTEMBER 12

Well, today it happened: I was running late for school, so my mom had to drive me. And before we left, she said, "It's getting cold out. Go put on another layer." So I went back to my room, and found that all my sweaters and sweatshirts were gone, except for the purple sweater-vest.

So I put it on, and planned to take it off as soon as I got to school.

Then, on the way into the school, I saw Jenny Bachman. I tried to hide so she wouldn't see me, but she looked over and said, "Hey! Nice sweater-vest!"

Argh. The only thing I hate more than when my mom forces me to wear stuff is when she's right.

SEPTEMBER 16 [mood: radioactive]

The Teenage Mutant Ninja Turtles are fun, but I bet that if you exposed turtles to radiation, they wouldn't suddenly gain a whole lot of martial-arts abilities. I bet they'd just get, like, covered with blisters and die.

Leonardo leads...

Donatello does machines...

Raphael is cool but crude...

Michelangelo is a party dude!

In bio class, we're learning about bacteria. On Thursday, Mr. Hamilton ran a swab across Leanne Chu's desk and then swiped it on a petri dish. Friday, he showed us all the bacteria that had grown on the dish overnight. It was pretty cool, but it totally freaked Leanne out. She showed up today

with a big bottle of Purell, and kept squirting it on her hands and staring at her desk like it was gonna attack her. Mr. Hamilton tried to calm her down and told her that there's bacteria on everything—even the food we eat. I don't think it worked, though. I saw her in the cafeteria later, closely examining a fish stick like she was looking for germs.

So today at school, Chuck was talking about this online game he's found, "Sword of the Valkyries." He says it's great—you can roam around ancient

Norway as a Viking and fight, like, other Vikings and dragons and stuff. So I just went on and created a new character for myself. I was going to just call him "Tad," but the name "Tad" was taken, and so was "Tadd." And so was "Ttad." And so was "Ttadd." So I wound up going with

"ViciousVikingSlayerTad3." ("ViciousVikingSlayer-Tad" and "ViciousVikingSlayerTad2" were taken.) I'm about to start playing—wish me luck!

Man, I'm tired. I started playing "Sword of the Valkyries" last night, and wound up joining a guild and going on a dungeon run. We found a baby

dragon, and all the other guild members already had one, so they let me keep him! I named him Fritz. Anyway, by the time it was all done, I looked up and it was two in the morning. Totally exhausted now. Going online to feed Fritz, then to sleep.

SEPTEMBER 20 [mood:  sleepier]

Sooooooooooo tired. When I went online to feed Fritz, some of the guild members asked if I wanted to go on a quest to get an immunity amulet, which I could totally use, because I keep getting killed whenever someone throws a cup of mead at me. (There's a lot of dangerous mead-throwing in "Sword of the Valkyries.")

So we went off and got one, and then the guild members said that since they'd helped me on my quest, I should help them go fight this wizard who's been harassing them. And I couldn't really say no, after they'd helped me get my amulet. So I'm not sure when I got to sleep, but I think the sun was rising. Just going to check in on the game now, and then I'm going to collapse.

Ugh. I'm in so much trouble right now. I stayed up till four last night playing "Sword of the Valkyries," and I really didn't feel like waking up and going to school this morning. So I told my folks I had a sore throat and a fever, and needed to sleep, and they let me stay home.

That would've worked out great, except that, when Sophie came home, she found me playing the game. The good news is, I convinced her not to tell Mom and Dad. The bad news is, in return, now I have to do pretty much whatever she says. I just spent an hour playing Uno with her, and in a few minutes, I have to go play Sorry! I also have to figure out a way to let her win, 'cause she gets mean when she loses.

My life officially sucks.

[mood: aggravated] **SEPTEMBER 22**

Grrr. ViciousVikingSlayerTad3 is dead. I was just about to go into battle when Sophie called me in to look under her bed for monsters, and by the time I was done, my character had been slain with a lightning bolt. So my guild kicked me out, on account of deadness. And then Sophie made me come into her room and kill a spider.

SEPTEMBER 23  [mood: annoyed]

If anyone reading this saw tonight's episode of *CSI*, could you please email me and let me know how it all turned out? Just before the episode ended, Sophie changed the channel to watch *SpongeBob SquarePants.* I was all ready to complain to Mom and Dad, but then Sophie said, "Are you sure you want to do that?"

So instead, I just went up to my room and drew pictures of SpongeBob being used as a sponge.

So last night, Sophie made me clean out her hamster's cage, and now, no matter how much I scrub, I smell like hamster. I thought it was just my imagination, but this morning in homeroom, Julie Underhill sniffed the air and said, "Ew . . . I smell something hamstery. I think it's Tad. Mrs. DeWitt, can I move?"

[mood: stressed] SEPTEMBER 25

7:04 p.m.:
I didn't think things could get worse, but now—BRB

7:06 p.m.:
they have, because—BRB

7:09 p.m.:
Sophie's got a little bell she rings whenever she—BRB

7:11 p.m.:
wants an Eskimo pie or a Fruit Roll-Up, which is surprisingly—BRB

7:14 p.m.:
often.

SEPTEMBER 26 [mood: relieved]

Today I had to give up going over to Chuck's house because Sophie insisted that I come to the tea party she was having with her stuffed animals. Which was bad enough, but then, when I got there, I found out that I wasn't even a guest—I was their waiter. So I had to keep on pouring fake tea for her teddy bear and elephant and

Robo Sapien, and Sophie kept complaining loudly to them that I was a really awful waiter, and saying that she wasn't going to tip me a dime.

After a half hour of this, I finally put the teapot down and went downstairs to Mom and Dad and told them that I'd faked being sick. I was expecting them to get mad and ground me or something, but instead, my dad just laughed and said, "We were wondering how much longer you could last." I guess my folks figured it out last week. As my mom put it, "We thought that having to be bossed around by Sophie was far worse than anything we could have done."

Anyway. I've got to go. I need to go tell Sophie about all the new monsters I've noticed under her bed.

SEPTEMBER 27 [mood:  surly]

I just got back from Best Buy, where they were selling a Special Edition DVD of *X-Men Origins: Wolverine*, with director's commentary. I think the only commentary I'd want to hear during *X-Men Origins: Wolverine* would be the director being poked with a stick, over and over, until he apologized for making a really crappy Wolverine movie.

SEPTEMBER 28 [mood: grossed out]

I don't get why some people think it's OK to leave their chewed-up gum in the drain of water fountains. It's really gross to have to stare at their gum when you're getting a drink of water. You know where I bet that doesn't happen? At the offices on *CSI*. I bet if someone did that at a CSI lab, they could examine the bite marks in the gum and then use dental records to match them up to the person who chewed it, and then force them to put it back in their mouth. At least, that's what I would do if I worked at a CSI lab.

October

Our whole family went to the zoo yesterday. And then, for Sophie, we went to the Children's Zoo. I don't understand the Children's Zoo. Like, isn't the whole zoo for children? It's not like the rest of the zoo is the Adult Zoo, where the bears swear and the giraffes smoke and the chimps serve hard liquor.

Anyway, Sophie really enjoyed the Children's Zoo, because they have machines where you can buy food and give it to the animals. She was having a lot of fun, feeding the pigs corn and giving each of them names like "Mr. Pigglesworth" and "Dr. Piggington." (Sophie's not very good at coming up with names.) And then my dad said to my mom, "Oh! This reminds me: When we get home, I've got to remember to defrost the pork chops for dinner." And Sophie said, "Why would a pig remind you to defrost pork chops?" And my dad kind of froze up and said, "Um, I don't know," which is weird, because the answer's pretty obvious. So I told Sophie, "Duh! Pork chops come from pigs." And then she screamed, and all the animals ran away, and she started crying, and we had to go home.

At dinner, Sophie refused to eat her pork chop. She just kept poking it with her fork and saying, "Poor Dr.

Piggington." I felt a little bad for her, but on the other hand: more pork chops for me.

Oh boy. Today, Sophie announced that she was going to be a vegetarian. She's not going to eat anything made from animals—no hamburgers, no steaks, no pork chops, no bacon. She's just going to eat chicken nuggets and vegetables. And then my mom pointed out that chicken nuggets are made from chickens, and Sophie kind of paused, but then she said, "OK, fine. I won't eat chicken nuggets, either, then." So tonight, we all had steak, and Sophie had cheese ravioli. She kept looking at us as we ate and saying "Moo" until my mom made her stop.

"MOOO."

For dinner tonight, my mom made turkey meat-loaf, and just as we were all getting ready to eat it, Sophie said, "I'm not eating turkey!" And my mom sighed and said, "Oh! You're still doing that?" And she had to get up and make Sophie some mac-and-cheese. Which would've been fine, but every once in a while, under her breath, Sophie would whisper, "Gobble-gobblegobblegobble." It sort of ruined dinner.

It was nice out tonight, so my dad grilled hot dogs and hamburgers for dinner, except for Sophie, who got a veggie burger and a Tofu Pup. She let me try a bite of each of them, and the nicest thing I can say about them is, size- and shape-wise, they're just like hot dogs and hamburgers. Taste-, texture-, and everything-else-wise, they're pretty much like kitchen sponges. Sophie tried to make us feel guilty while she was eating, by saying "Woof!" and "Oink!"— which confused my parents for a little while. But then they explained to her that hot dogs and ham- burgers don't have any dogs or ham in them, and she started mooing.

OCTOBER 5   [mood: fishy]

Sophie's vegetarianism is beginning to annoy everyone. I could tell, because my mom made fish for dinner, and as she served it, she announced, "You know what noise a fish makes? None. Fish don't make any noise at all." Then she gave Sophie some beans and rice. But I'll give Sophie credit: She ate her dinner really fast, then said, "May I be excused?" and went into the family room to watch

Finding Nemo with the volume turned all the way up. My mom just rolled her eyes and said, "We've got to do something about this."

OCTOBER 6 [mood: glad]

This morning, there was a nice surprise for breakfast: My mom made bacon for everyone. We all had some, except for Sophie, who got cold cereal. Which was too bad for her, because she loooooooves bacon. And then my mom said, "Oh! I accidentally made enough for four of us by mistake! I'll just put the extra over here," and put it down next to Sophie. I could see her looking at it all through breakfast, and it was driving her nuts. And finally, she said, "You know what? I bet not all pigs are nice. Maybe some pigs are really mean. And maybe some pigs deserve to die." And then she started shoving the bacon in her mouth.

Afterward, my mom and dad and I all agreed that it was a little scary and a little creepy. But, on the plus side, she's not going to be mooing or oinking during dinner anymore, and that's a really good thing.

Went to the mall today and walked by the Build-a-Bear Workshop. I don't understand why anyone goes there. The mall has, like, three toy stores in it, where you can buy bears that've already been built.

[mood: nervous] **OCTOBER 8**

In homeroom this morning, Jerry Baxter leaned over and told me the big news: His older sister is friends with Megan March's older sister, and his sister told him that Megan March had a sleepover at her place, and all the girls who were there made a list, grading all the eighth-grade boys on cuteness, from A to F. Jerry said that he got an A-minus, which isn't too bad. I asked him where I was ranked, and he said he didn't know—all he knows is that he got an A-minus.

I told Chuck about the list, and he started telling other people, and by lunchtime,

A-the list was pretty much the only thing anyone was talking about. Ryan Pendleton finally said, "This is stupid—we don't even know if there is a list or not." And then he walked over to Megan and said, "So Jerry Baxter gets an A-minus, huh?" And she said, "I don't know what you're talking about." And he said, "The list you made at your sleepover? Grading boys on cuteness?" And she said, "We never made a list. And also: Jerry Baxter didn't get an A-minus."

So there's definitely a list. Now I just need to find out where I am on it.

Not yet rated!

Today, we all spent another day just trying to find out where we stand on the list. Chuck says that he spent a while talking to Ingrid Grant, who was at the sleepover, and she told him that he got a B-plus, but that she'd wanted to give him an A. I asked him if he found out what I got, but he said that he was a little too distracted.

On the bus ride home today, Doug Spivak leaned over and told me that someone had posted the grade list on the wall of the girls' bathroom. I asked him if he'd seen what my grade was, and he said he hadn't, but that he'd gotten a C-plus. And I was about to say something like, "Well, look, it's just a stupid list," when he said, "Pretty sweet, right? It's the best grade I've ever gotten in anything."

I guess, in some ways, it must be nice to be Doug Spivak.

Before school today, I tried to go into the girls' bathroom, but it was never empty. And I tried again at lunch, and the same thing happened. That's when I realized that I couldn't go in there when everyone else was out and around in the hallways, which left me with only one option. During English, I went up to Mrs. White and whispered, "I have diarrhea," and she let me go to the bathroom during class. So I sneaked into the girls' bathroom and took a look at the list.

And my name's not on it.

Billy Maguire

NO WAY!

B-Minus!

I checked and double-checked, and it's not there. Every other guy in our class is on the list. Billy Maguire is on the list, and he moved away two years ago! But I'm not on there, and I don't know why. Is it because I'm too ugly to grade? Because they're angry with me for some reason? It's driving me crazy—I'd almost rather have a bad grade than no grade at all.

Well, this morning, before class, I went over to Megan's locker and asked, as casually as I could, "Hey, Megan: I know there's a list. I saw it in the girls' bathroom. Why am I not on it?" And she said the worst three words she could possibly say:

"Who are you?"

And I said, "I'm Tad." And she said, "Oh. Right! Tad. Yeah, sorry. We just forgot about you."

I've gone to school with Megan since kindergarten. We were paired up in the "buddy system" for a full day for our class trip to the state capitol in sixth grade. I can't believe I was forgotten.

I'm going to have to try and be more memorable.

I've come up with a great plan to get more people to remember who I am. I realized that I need something to make me stand out, so I've decided that I'm going to start wearing a hat all the time. I'm going to be the hat-wearing guy. Maybe I'll even get a nickname, like "Cap Boy" or something. I'm trying it out tomorrow—wish me luck!

Bad news: Turns out, it's against the school rules to wear a hat all the time.

But tomorrow, I've got a great plan: I'm going to be the kid who always wears funny buttons to school. I got one that says VISUALIZE WHIRLED PEAS, and I'm going to wear it all day tomorrow.

Guess what? It's also against the rules to wear buttons to school.

But I'm not giving up. Now I've got a foolproof plan: I'm going to wear sunglasses everywhere. I've even figured out what my nickname should be: "Shades." This has got to work.

Well, it turns out that it's really hard to see indoors when you're wearing sunglasses—so for instance, you might not see the door to the faculty lounge opening until it hits you in the face. I got a bloody nose, and my sunglasses broke. Dr. Evans said she was really sorry, but I should know better than to wear sunglasses indoors.

After school, Chuck told me that it might be time to stop trying to come up with ways to be memorable. As he said, "Right now, you're going to

be remembered as the guy who keeps getting in trouble for wearing things." He had a point.

I've never understood why Batman has villains named the Joker *and* the Riddler—there's not a huge difference between a joke and a riddle. I bet they both would get super sensitive if you pointed out the similarities, though. I bet if you brought up the Riddler around the Joker, he'd be like, "No, no, we're totally different! Sure, we both hate Batman. But he only uses the kind of humor that's question-and-answer-based, and mine is more of a prank-type thing!"

In bio class today, Mr. Hamilton made us dissect mice. Seema Gupta refused to do it, because she said that she had a mouse at home named Buttons and she wouldn't be able to dissect a mouse without thinking of him. But Mr. Hamilton said that if she refused, she'd get an F on the assignment. That's when Seema suddenly remembered that Buttons was a gerbil, not a mouse, and so she'd have no problem doing the assignment.

Mr. Hamilton kept walking around the room, saying things like, "See if you can find the squeaky part" and "Save the tail—it's a delicacy!" At one point, he held up two of the dead mice like they were puppets and pretended they were talking to each other.

I used to wonder why whenever our family went out to dinner at Applebee's, I'd always see

Mr. Hamilton there, eating alone. But I think I've figured out why.

Today at lunch, Jenny Bachman came over to my table and invited me to her Halloween party! Actually, she invited everyone at the table. I think she invited everyone in our class. But still: I got invited to a party at Jenny Bachman's house! And it's a costume party, so I have to come up with something that'll impress her.

I told my parents about the party at dinner, and my mom was like, "Oooh, a Halloween party! Why don't you just reuse one of your old costumes? We have some makeup—you could go as a clown! You did that in third grade, and you were so cute! Or a cat—remember the year you went as a cat? I think we still have your ears!" And I said, "Mom! It's a party at a girl's house!" And then she said, "Oh! Right. So I guess you don't want to go as Cookie Monster again, either, huh?"

OCTOBER 24  [mood: stumped]

Chuck and I spent most of lunch today trying to think of a good costume. It needs to be cool and creative, and it can't have a mask, because I want Jenny to be able to see my face. And it has to be something we both can do, so that if people think it's stupid, there's at least one other person at the party who's dressed equally stupidly. We finally decided that we'd both go as vampires, because girls seem to really, really like vampires. But Chuck just called me and said that his mom won't let him go as a vampire, because she's afraid he could swallow his vampire teeth and choke.

It's not easy being Chuck.

[mood:  happy] OCTOBER 25

Chuck had an awesome idea today: He's got a black suit from his Bar Mitzvah, and I've got the one we bought when Great-Aunt Sophie died. We just need to wear black ties and sunglasses, and we can be Men in Black! Chuck is a genius.

OCTOBER 26  [mood: confused]

I got in trouble tonight at dinner, and I'm still not sure why. Sophie went to the mall with my parents today and picked out her Halloween costume—she's going as Sleeping Beauty. And all I said was, "Y'know, I don't understand why the prince would want to kiss Sleeping Beauty, because she's been lying there for a really long time, so I bet she stinks. I mean, there's no way that, after lying there for all that time, she hasn't peed herself." And Sophie started to cry and say that she didn't want to be the princess who smelled like pee, and that she wanted a different costume, and my mom announced that I wouldn't be allowed to watch TV tonight.

[mood: annoyed] OCTOBER 27

In trouble again. My parents went to the mall and got Sophie a Little Mermaid costume, and all I said was, "You won't be able to say 'Trick or treat.' The Little Mermaid gave away her voice in order to get legs, remember?" And Sophie said that she didn't want to go the whole night without speaking, so she'd have to get a different costume, and I had my Wii taken away.

Sorry I didn't write yesterday. My parents took my computer away after they came back with a third costume for Sophie, a Cinderella costume, and I said that it was a really pretty dress, given that it had been sewn together by mice and rats.

I need to learn to keep my mouth shut.

OCTOBER 30 [mood: pensive]

Sophie's getting ready for Halloween—she's been practicing saying "Trick or treat!" really loud. I don't understand why we still say "Trick or treat."

Nobody actually bothers to trick the people who don't give them candy, so the whole "trick" part of "Trick or treat" is just an empty threat, and everyone knows it. I think the "trick" part is just there because it makes it sound like you're offering people an option—it just seems rude to knock on people's doors and shout, "Treat!"

[mood: blue]   **OCTOBER 31**

6:15 p.m.

Jenny's party is two hours away, and I can't get in touch with Chuck. He wasn't in school today, and he's not answering his phone. Meanwhile, my mom and dad just took Sophie trick-or-treating. Sophie finally settled on going as an angel, and Mom and Dad got kind of mad at me when I looked at her costume and said, "You know, another way of looking at it is that you're going as a dead kid," and Sophie started to cry. My mom and dad only got her to stop by promising to take her trick-or-treating over in the super-rich neighborhood where people give out full-size candy bars.

6:37 p.m.

Just got a text message from Chuck. He's got strep throat, so he won't be able to be the other Man in Black. Which kind of ruins the whole plan, because the Men in Black thing only works if there's more than one of you. If it's just you, you look like a funeral director. Now I don't have anything to wear to Jenny's party.

7:21 p.m.

I just had a great idea! I remembered Jenny saying once how much she loved the movie *Avatar*, and how she thought the guy from it was really cute! I dug around in the attic and found the blue makeup from when I was Cookie Monster. I covered my face and arms in blue makeup and put some yellow dots on it, and I borrowed the wig that Sophie wore when she went as Hannah Montana two years ago—it's not bad, if I do say so myself. I'm off to the party now—wish me luck!

9:40 p.m.

Ugh. Bad night. I got to Jenny Bachman's house, and she seemed sort of startled when she opened the door and I was standing there. She was like, "Are you a Smurf?" And I said, "No! I'm a Na'vi! Like from one of your favorite movies, *Avatar*?" And she said, "Oh! Right!" And then her mom saw me and said, "That's blue makeup?" And I said, "Yep!" And her mom said, "I'm sorry, but please don't sit on any of our furniture. Or touch our walls. OK?"

So I stood around for a few minutes near the punch bowl, and saw what everyone else had come as—a lot of people weren't even wearing costumes, and the ones who were, were wearing really simple ones, like the guy who'd stapled some socks to himself and come as Static Cling.

And then it got even worse: I saw Mark O'Keefe, who was there dressed as Wolverine, with his arm around Jenny Bachman.

After that, I decided I didn't want to stick around anymore, and I

started walking home. I was halfway home when my parents drove by, and my mom rolled down the window and said, "Tad? Is that you?" And I said, "Yeah." And my dad said, "Weren't you going as one of the Men in Black?" And I said, "Chuck got sick." And then my sister said, "Is that my Hannah Montana wig?" And I said, "Maybe." My mom said, "We'd offer you a ride home, but . . . you know . . . the car's upholstery." So I walked the rest of the way home.

Now I'm in my room. I washed as much of the blue off as I could, but I keep finding more, like in my ears or on my neck. Sophie just came to the door and said, "Tad? I'm sorry you had a bad time at your party. You can have one of my Snickerses if you want." Which was really nice of her. I mean, she's allergic to peanuts, so I'm not sure why she didn't let me have all the Snickers. But still . . . it was nice of her.

November

Well, there's good news and bad news: The good news is, I'm now very memorable—everyone in school knows who I am, and I even have a nickname.

The bad news is, the nickname is "Smurf."

I guess everybody found out about my *Avatar* costume from the other night. I can even hear people whispering "Smurf" when I walk down the hallway. The only nice part about the whole day was when Jenny Bachman came over to me and said, "Tad! I'm sorry you didn't stick around the other night. I don't care what anyone else says—I thought your costume was really cool." Which was really nice of her, and almost made up for the fact that our conversation ended with Mark O'Keefe coming over, saying, "Let's go!" and then, as they walked away, adding, "Later, Smurf."

NOVEMBER 3 [mood: confused]

Sophie just got back from her best friend Stacy's birthday party at Chuck E. Cheese. I wonder what the meeting was like where they decided on that restaurant's mascot. Like, did anyone pipe up and go, "Hey, maybe we shouldn't have our mascot be a six-foot-tall rat"? Or was everyone just OK with it?

[mood: happy] **NOVEMBER 4**

Today's the end of Daylight Savings Time, and like I do every year, I accidentally set my watch forward, instead of backward, so I spent most of the day two hours off. I always get that "Spring forward, fall back" thing wrong, because it seems like, if you've just sprung forward, then you're more likely to fall forward. Go ahead—try it. Jump forward and see which way you fall.

See?

That's why I've been trying to come up with my own way to remember how Daylight Savings works. Here's one:

"Coiled springs hold lots of power, go ahead and add an hour.

When you fall, you'll hurt your back, so an hour you should subtract."

I realize that one's a little long, though. Here's a shorter one I came up with:

"Spring flowers? Add an hour.

Fall snacks? An hour back."

I know that the "snacks" part doesn't make sense. I'm still working on it.

NOVEMBER 5 [mood: thoughtful]

We're studying Greek myths in class now. Today, we learned about Medusa, whose face could turn anyone who looked at it into stone. What I can't figure out is how everyone discovered that fact.

It's not like you could *see* Medusa turn someone into stone—if you were there, then you were
turned into stone, too. And if you weren't there,
and showed up later, how would you be able to
figure out that the reason all your friends were
now statues was that they'd looked at Medusa? I
guess maybe, one time, someone was in the next
room when his friends went in to see Medusa, and
his friends shouted something like, "Here comes
Medusa! She's coming this way! She's rounding
the corner! We're just about to see her! Oh, wow,
she's hideou—" And then the guy figured out, after
the fact, "Oh, looking at Medusa turns you into
stone."

Yeah. That must be what happened.

NOVEMBER 7 [mood: absentminded]

My dad's been teaching me to play chess. It's a strange game. I kind of can't concentrate on playing it, because I just keep picturing this weird kingdom where castles keep moving sideways, bishops are always walking diagonally, and horses can only gallop in L-shapes.

[mood: bored] ## NOVEMBER 8

I was flipping around on cable today and caught a bit of *Star Trek: The Next Generation* and then some of the last movie they did, and y'know what? That robot got old.

Then
(Such technology!)

Now
(Robotic wonder!)

Today in class, they passed out the order forms for school pictures. I brought it home, and my mom said, "Well, Tad, you want to give it another try this year?"

I have a bad history with school pictures. I've never gotten a good one. In first grade, I got distracted by a noise when the picture was taken, so it's just a blurry picture of the back of my head. In second grade, I was chewing on my pen that morning and it burst open, so my face is covered with a big ink blot. In third grade, I sneezed right when the camera went off. In fourth grade, I wore a shirt the same color as the background, so it looks like a picture of a floating head. In fifth grade, I had the hiccups when the picture was taken, so I'm all blurry. In sixth grade, I had an allergic reaction to the free comb the photographer gave everyone, and my eyes got so puffy, I could barely see. In seventh grade, I had a bloody nose earlier that day, so my shirt is covered in blood. (My dad calls the photo "your mug shot.") So at this point, my mom just checks the box for the smallest package of photos they offer—one 5 x 3 photo and four wallet-sized photos. "If they're good, we'll order more," she said.

But this is going to be the year I have a good school picture. I can just feel it. I'm going to get a haircut this weekend, and it's going to look great.

First Grade   Second Grade   Third Grade

Fourth Grade   Fifth Grade   Sixth Grade

Seventh Grade

Stupid Supercuts. I went to get my hair cut today, and at first it was really nice, 'cause there was a TV above the barber's chair, so I could watch it while my barber cut my hair. It was only toward the end of the haircut that I realized my barber was watching the TV, too. So instead of what I asked for—which was short on the sides and long on top—I got a haircut that was short on the left side and long on the right. It made my head look lopsided. It was so bad, the only thing I could do was ask the barber to take the clippers and make it short all over. I also asked him to turn off the TV while he did it.

Anyway. Now I have a buzz cut. It's OK, though—I'll just wear a hat in my photo.

[mood: embarrassed] **NOVEMBER 13**

Well, there are two bad things about my new haircut: One, my head is really, really cold. And two, as June Chen pointed out in front of everyone today at lunch, without much hair on my head, you can totally see that I have a huge unibrow. She said I look like Bert from *Sesame Street*, which would be mean if it weren't kind of true.

I've got to fix this before Friday.

NOVEMBER 14 [mood: embarrassed-er]

Here is some advice: If you are going to try to get rid of a unibrow, don't just take a razor and shave down the middle of it, because you'll probably cut

off more than you mean to, and then you'll try to even it up on one side, and then you'll realize you cut too much on that side and need to even it up on the other side, and one thing will lead to another and then you'll have no eyebrows.

NOVEMBER 15 [mood: embarrassed-er-er]

Here is some more advice: If you've semi-accidentally shaved your eyebrows off, don't try to draw them on with a Sharpie, because even if you do a really good job, people will notice and make fun of you. Also, it takes forever to wash your fake eyebrows off.

So today was picture day, and I showed up wearing a baseball cap and sunglasses. The photographer told me I wasn't allowed to wear them in the picture, so I took them off. And then he looked at me and said, "Do you have some sort of a disease?" And I said, "No. I have a bad haircut and I shaved off my eyebrows sort of by accident."

And he leaned over and whispered, "Um . . . do you want me to accidentally leave the lens cap on for your photo?" And I said, "That'd be great." So here's how I'll look in this year's yearbook:

Eighth Grade

The sad thing is, I think it may be my best school photo ever.

 [mood: hungry] **NOVEMBER 18**

"Two scoops of raisins" sounds really impressive until you realize that they never say how big the scoops are. What if the scoops are super tiny, and only hold one raisin each?

In biology today, we learned that raccoons are nocturnal animals, so if you see one in daylight, it probably has rabies. Then, when I got home, Sophie was watching *Pocahontas*. It really changes that movie if, the whole time, you keep thinking, "Man, that raccoon's *totally* going to bite her face off any second now."

You know who I feel bad for? The second-to-last airbender. Because I bet he was probably really good at bending air, and nobody ever even talks about him.

I wonder how seals got to be named "seals," while sea lions got the name "sea lion." "Sea lion" is such a better name than "seal." I like to imagine that when all the animals were picking out names, the seals went first, and they said, "We want to be called seals!" And they were pretty happy with

that, until the sea lions' turn came, and they were like, "We're going with 'sea lions'!" And the seals were all like, "Wait: You can do that? Just choose a cool animal and put 'sea' in front of it? Can we be sea eagles?" But the animal-naming committee was like, "It's too late, we've moved on to these guys over here. What do you want to be called?" And the sea horses were like, "Sea horses!"

NOVEMBER 22 [mood: thankful]

Today was Thanksgiving, and I'm stuffed with turkey. Dinner was good: My aunt Pam and uncle Owen came over, and my mom made turkey and cranberry sauce and stuffing and green-bean casserole and sweet potatoes, all of which I hate eating on any day of the year but Thanksgiving. I guess Thanksgiving's supposed to be just like the first meal the Pilgrims ate with the Native Americans, but I'm not sure whether the Pilgrims or the Native Americans brought the marshmallows for the sweet potatoes or the canned onions for the green-bean casserole.

After dinner, my uncle Owen said, "Do you want to play a little football?" So I went into the living room, turned on the Wii, and put in Madden NFL, but it turned out, he wanted to play real football, with, like, a ball in the yard. I'd never really thrown a football around much before. It's kind of hard, and boring, and there are no cheat codes to help you throw it better. I don't get the point of it.

NOVEMBER 24 [mood:  irritable]

I don't get why they're Alvin and the Chipmunks. Alvin *is* a chipmunk. It should be Alvin and the Two Other Chipmunks. Or maybe The Three Chipmunks.

(I know it's not the biggest logical problem in a movie about three singing chipmunks. But still, it bothers me.)

[mood: thirsty] **NOVEMBER 26**

Today, I got into an argument with Chuck about how to pronounce "Minute Maid," as in "Minute Maid orange juice." I said it's pronounced "min-itt," as in, the thing that there are sixty of in an hour, and he said it's pronounced "mih-nyoot," as in, something that's really tiny. I told him that was stupid, and why would anyone name their orange juice for a tiny cleaning woman? And he said, well, if it's pronounced "minute" as in "a minute of time," then what's a "minute maid"? Someone who cleans up after you, but only for sixty seconds?

I hate to admit it, but he sort of had a point.

NOVEMBER 28 [mood:  cold]

This morning, I saw my neighbor Mr. Baxter packing up his car for a trip. He said he was going to drive up to the lake this weekend to go ice fishing, which is weird, because it's pretty easy to make ice at home.

December

There's a weekend-long James Bond marathon on TV, and I watched some of it with my dad today. Here's what I wonder about James Bond: I get that he has a license to kill. But what do you have to go through to get it? I like to think that first, you have to have a learner's permit to kill. Like, you can go around killing people, but your mom or dad have to come with you. And then maybe there's a written portion, where you have to answer a lot of multiple-choice questions about when it is and isn't okay to kill. And if they catch you killing while you're drunk, they can take away your license, and then you have to ask a friend to do all your killing for you. That must suck.

I watched a little more James Bond with my dad. It cracks me up that one of the villains is this guy:

Because if he's got a cat on his lap, that means that somewhere nearby in his evil lair, there's got to be a litter box.

In social studies, we're learning about how America got started from thirteen colonies. I can't believe anyone would start a country with thirteen of anything— it's just unlucky. If you ask me, they should've either added a colony or kicked one of them out—probably Delaware.

Today in social studies, Mr. Rao started off by telling us that today is the sixty-fifth anniversary of Pearl Harbor. Doug Spivak raised his hand and said that *Pearl Harbor* came out in the summer, but Mr. Rao explained that he was talking about the actual attack on Pearl Harbor, not the movie. And then Doug said, "Wait: The stuff in *Pearl*

Harbor really happened?" And Mr. Rao said yes, it really happened. And Doug said, "Well, what about *Armageddon*? Did that really happen, too?" And Mr. Rao said no, that one was fake.

And so then for about five minutes, Doug listed movies, and Mr. Rao told him whether the stuff in them really happened or not. (*Zorro*: No. *The Alamo*: Yes. *Saving Private Ryan*: Yes and no. *Pirates of the Caribbean*: No. *Dodgeball*: No. *National Treasure*: No.) When Doug asked about *Raiders of the Lost Ark*, Mr. Rao refused to answer any more questions.

DECEMBER 8 [mood:  grossed out]

If you think about it, *tater tot* is a bad name for a food, because it suggests that you're eating potato babies.

[mood: inquisitive] DECEMBER 9

It's a Wonderful Life is on TV today. If it's true that every time a bell rings, an angel gets its wings, then I don't understand why Clarence goes to so much trouble to help Jimmy Stewart. It seems like he could just as easily get his wings the next time a handbell choir performs.

DECEMBER 11 [mood: puzzled]

I really don't understand why any baseball team would choose to name themselves the Anaheim Angels. That's like calling yourself "the Anaheim Dead People."

There was an assembly today where we all had to listen to the kids in the choir sing Christmas songs, plus one Hanukkah song and one song about Kwanzaa. They sang "Rudolph, the Red-Nosed Reindeer," and I started thinking about the reindeer games they wouldn't let Rudolph play. What kind of games would reindeer play? They walk around on all four of their limbs, so it's not like they can catch or throw anything. And they certainly can't play tag, because their antlers are so

pointy. I suppose they could play board games or something, so long as they could pick up their play-ing pieces with their mouths and maybe throw the dice by roll-ing them around in their mouths and spit-ting them out. If that's what they were doing,

I don't feel all that sorry for Rudolph, because board games are kind of lame.

In English class, we read the story "The Gift of the Magi," which is about this woman who sells her hair to buy her husband a watch chain for Christmas—only he's sold his watch to buy her combs for her hair. And the moral of the story is that it's better to give than to receive, although to me, the bigger news in the story is, some people buy hair. That's so weird.

I've been thinking about it, and I think a good story would be "The Birthday Gift of the Magi." It's about a woman who sells her hair to buy her husband a watch chain, and he's like, "Oh, hey . . . thanks,"

and then he doesn't give her anything, because it's not her birthday. And they both just sort of sit there, feeling kind of awkward.

DECEMBER 15 [mood: anxious]

We're doing Secret Santa in my homeroom. We picked names yesterday, and I got Aaron Reynolds, who used to beat me up and give me wedgies in elementary school. Luckily, Chuck got Patricia Ortiz, who I've kind of liked since sixth grade, and he agreed to swap names with me. So now I have to figure out what to get Patricia that:

A) she'll really like, and

B) costs under $10, 'cause that's the limit they set.

Which sucks, 'cause you can't really get anyone anything good for ten bucks. Chuck pointed out that you can get ten small chilis at Wendy's for $10, but I don't think that's the sort of thing you want to unwrap from your Secret Santa.

Chuck's mom took us to the mall today so we could find our Secret Santa stuff. I was thinking of getting Patricia a tiny bottle of perfume or something, but I couldn't find any bottles that didn't cost, like, eight times what we're allowed to spend. Also, the salespeople at JCPenney were spraying samples on people, and Chuck kept getting hit by them, so he really wanted to leave. I can't blame

him. He was beginning to smell like one of my mom's magazines.

We went through the rest of the mall and didn't find anything for Patricia, but at Best Buy, Chuck found a discount bin of $10 DVDs, so we tried to find the one Aaron Reynolds was least likely to want. I hope he enjoys *Legally Blonde 2: Red, White and Blonde*.

DECEMBER 18 [mood: nervous]

After school, Chuck and I went downtown to do more shopping. We didn't find anything for Patricia, and we looked everywhere—even Victoria's Secret. Actually, we didn't really think we'd find anything for Patricia there—we just liked having an excuse to see what the inside of the store was like.

I asked if they could help me find something for one of my classmates, and the saleslady said, "Is this your girlfriend?" and I said, "No, just a girl in my class." And the saleslady said, "There is nothing here you should buy for her."

DECEMBER 19 [mood:  excited]

So tomorrow's the Secret Santa exchange, and I really needed to buy Patricia's gift today, so Chuck and I had his older sister take us to the super-nice mall on the other side of town. I wound up getting her present at the Godiva chocolate place. The smallest box they had was $15, but it looked tiny and only had, like, three chocolates in it, so I wound up getting her the one that costs $30. It's more than I'm spending on any member of my family, but then again, I don't really want to ask any of them out.

[mood:  annoyed] DECEMBER 20

Today was the big gift exchange. We all dropped our presents in a box, and then they were handed out. Chuck got a copy of the third Harry Potter book, which had clearly been read by whoever gave it to him. I got a note saying that my Santa didn't have time to buy anything, and that he'd give me $10 later. Meanwhile, Patricia opened up her present and was all like, "Oh, chocolate! Great! Someone's trying to make me break out and get fat." So Aaron offered to swap his DVD with her. And she was all, "Oh, that's so sweet of you! I love this movie! Thank you so so so so much!" And then it came time for everyone to tell each other who their Secret Santa was, and I told Patricia, and she kind of

said, "Uh-huh," and went back to talking to Aaron.

And as if that weren't depressing enough, after homeroom, I walked by Jenny Bachman's locker, and she was showing off the neck-lace that Mark O'Keefe had gotten her.

One of these days, I'm going to write a

story called "The Gift of the Tadi." It's about how it's better to give than to receive, but sometimes, it just sucks all around.

Great news! Jenny Bachman broke up with Mark O'Keefe!

I guess she was wearing her necklace at the mall, and then she saw, like, two girls from other middle schools wearing the exact same necklace, and she asked them where they'd gotten it, and all three of them thought they were dating Mark!

This may be the best Christmas gift I've ever gotten.

OK, I realize it's not the point of the story, but still: If I were Scrooge, and I got to see Christmas Future, I'd try and snag a newspaper while I was there so I could place bets on sports and win a lot of money.

It's Christmas Eve. My mom and dad just gave Sophie and me our night-before-Christmas presents, which are—as always—pajamas. My pajamas have pockets in the pants. I'm not sure why. I guess so I have someplace to put whatever I pick up in my dreams?

[mood: merry] DECEMBER 25

Christmas was fun. My parents got me some aftershave and some books and video games and a new sweater-vest, and Grandma Judy sent me some Lego blocks, I guess because she still thinks of me as being seven years old. Sophie got some accounting software and a real grown-up accounts-receivable ledger, which is exactly what she wanted. She also put on a really good show of pretending to be excited because Santa had come for a visit, which made my parents happy.

DECEMBER 26 [mood:  sleepy]

According to the calendar, today is something called "Boxing Day" in England. I hoped that meant that the whole country took part in a big fistfight, but apparently, it's just what they call the day after Christmas there.

[mood: disgusted] DECEMBER 27

It snowed yesterday, so Sophie and I went to the park and made a snowman. Here is some advice, if you're thinking about making a snowman: Make sure you don't do it in the part of the park where dogs tend to poop a lot. We got about halfway through rolling one big snowball when we figured out why our snowman smelled so bad.

Tonight, my mom made me sit down and write a thank-you note to Grandma Judy for the Legos she sent me. I felt stupid writing out the words "Thanks for the Legos—I look forward to playing with them," but my mom insisted it was the polite thing to do. But when I asked if she was going to send a thank-you note for the talking bathroom scale that Grandma Judy got for her, she said, "None of your business."

Well, it's the last day of the year, which always makes me a little sad. Looking back on the past year, it was pretty OK. I got most of my New Year's resolutions done: I created my blog, I started shaving, I learned how to do at least half a kickflip, and I technically *did* get some girls to notice me, even if it was just to call me "Smurf."

And next year might be a good year. I went down to the mall today to exchange the Lego blocks for a Wii game, and I ran into Jenny Bachman. I told her I was sorry to hear that she and Mark O'Keefe had broken up, and she said it was OK, she didn't have much in common with him anyway. Then she asked if maybe I wanted to go ice-skating with her sometime, and I said sure. So we made a plan for next Saturday.

So things might be looking up for me. I feel like good things might be about to happen. I'm excited, I'm hopeful, and I'm very very nervous.

Because I have no idea how to ice-skate.

Tim Carvell is the head writer for *The Daily Show with Jon Stewart,* for which he has won five Emmys. He has also served as a writer and editor at *Fortune, Sports Illustrated Women,* and *Entertainment Weekly.* His work has also appeared in *New York* magazine, the *New York Times, Esquire, Slate,* and *McSweeney's*; the *Daily Show* books *America: The Book* and *Earth: The Book*; and the anthologies *More Mirth of a Nation, Created in Darkness by Troubled Americans,* and *The McSweeney's Joke Book of Joke Books.* He lives in New York with his partner, Tom Keeton.